Praise for
bestsell

***The Genie's Double Trouble***

"The story is unique, intriguing and I couldn't put it down."—Goodreads

***Courting the Cat Whisperer***

"I loved the storytelling + the characters. It has all the ingredients that you need for a great book!"—Goodreads

***The Yin to His Yang***

"Pick up your copy and find out what happens. Have a few giggles along the way."—Book Nook Nuts

"This was a well put together story of multidimensional characters with complex relationships."—The BookChick

"Filled with humor, a bit of suspense, and whole lot of romance this is sure to appeal to many readers."—A Cozy Booknook

"…delightfully cute, and extremely entertaining! I think I had a goofy smile on my face the majority of the time that I read it."—Beyond the Pages

"…I just can't put into words how great this book is."—Lisa Bateman

"Great read! It is a compelling book! Couldn't put it down. On my way to the next one…tempted by the excerpt in the back of this one."—Judith L. Marshall

# Books by Wynter Daniels

*A Witch in Time*
*Her Homerun Hottie*
*Beauty and the Bigfoot Hunter*
*Burning Touch* and *Tropic of Trouble*
*Chasing the Stag*
*Courting the Cat Whisperer*
*Emerald Intrigue*
*Employee Relations*
*Game of Smoke and Mirrors*
*Protective Custody*
*Shades of Sexy*
*The Best Man's Proposal*:
*The Fortuneteller's Folly*
*The Genie's Double Trouble*
*The Surrogate Husband*
*The Yin to His Yang*:

*The Witches of Freedom Moon* Series
*Hidden Magic* (Book One)
*Killer Magic* (Book Two)
*Dream Magic* (Book Three)

Boxed Sets
*The Witches of Freedom Moon*

# Gambling on the Artist

by

Wynter Daniels

Copyright © 2019 by Wynter Daniels

All rights reserved. No part of this book may be reproduced in any form or by any electronic or mechanical means, including information storage and retrieval systems—except in the case of brief quotations embodied in critical articles or reviews—without permission in writing from the author.

This book is a work of fiction. All characters, events, scenes, plots and associated elements remain the exclusive copyrighted and/or trademarked property of CPC Publishing, LLC. Any similarity to real persons, living or dead, is purely coincidental and not intended by the author or CPC Publishing.

Published in the United States of America.

Cover design: Dar Albert, Wicked Smart Designs

ISBN: 9781080979417

eBook ASIN: B07VGKMHN4

# Welcome to Cat's Paw Cove!

Dear Reader,

Cat's Paw Cove is a fictional, magical town where anything is possible! It was dreamed up by Wynter Daniels and Catherine Kean and is located south of St. Augustine on Florida's Atlantic coast. The name Cat's Paw Cove is derived from the small islands in the harbor, which look like the pads of a cat's paw.

We are so excited to bring you not only our own stories, but also contributions from an incredibly talented group of Guest Authors. With paranormal and mystery romances, historicals, time travels, and more, there's something for everyone.

We hope you'll enjoy reading the series as much as we enjoy writing it. For more information about the Cat's Paw Cove series, please visit:
**http://CatsPawCoveRomance.com**.

You are also welcome to join our fun, friendly Facebook group where you can interact with the authors, learn about our upcoming book releases and special events, and more:
**https://www.facebook.com/groups/CatsPawCove/**

Happy reading!

Wynter Daniels and Catherine Kean

# Prologue

Pain exploded through Eli Kincaid's left side. Another hard kick to his ribs and he was seeing stars. Two beefy arms lifted him to his feet then forced Eli into the back seat of a black Escalade behind the casino in Atlantic City. The blond giant—one of the men who'd just beaten the snot out of him—slid in next to Eli.

Rodrigo Diaz jabbed a finger at him from the other side of the leather seat. "Were you trying to skip out on what you owe me?"

"Nah," Eli said. "I was just heading out for some saltwater taffy. I hear it's pretty good."

Rodrigo smirked. "Smart asses don't impress me, Mr. Kincaid."

"Darn it." Eli shrugged. "How about sprinters? Do they impress you? Tell you what. You let me out, and I'll show you what a great runner I am."

The other thug, a huge dark-haired dude with a pink scar across his cheek—who was almost as big as the blond—got into the driver's seat of the SUV and pulled away from the hotel.

"Not likely," Rodrigo replied.

Eli's heartbeat thudded in his ears. Were they taking him somewhere to kill him? The sharp stabbing in his side was so intense that he could barely breathe. He probably had at least two broken ribs, maybe more. "Seriously, though, I was just going out for some breakfast. I had every intention of paying you what I owe you, Mr. Diaz, I swear." The words sounded cheap as tin, even to him.

The blond dude let out a snicker. "So you always take your suitcase and laptop with you to breakfast? I seen you put them in the trunk of your car."

Damn, he should have figured that Rodrigo had been having him watched. "I never leave home without them. Not that the hotel is home, but you know what I mean."

The blond grabbed a fistful of Eli's shirt and snarled at him. "One more smart crack and I'll give you another black eye to match the one you already got."

Eli gulped. "Got it."

"You'll have to forgive my associates," Rodrigo told Eli. "Sven and Manny aren't usually so inclined to violence."

Yeah, right. The brutes had seemed pretty inclined to hurt him.

"Sven's been watching you since last night," Rodrigo continued. "I was hoping you wouldn't disappear before we could settle our business, but it appears that was exactly what you were trying to do."

He wiped his sweaty hands on his pants. How could he have known when Rodrigo had invited him into a private game of Texas Holdem that the diminutive senior citizen was actually a shark? Not that Eli had planned to stiff the guy—not then, at least. Running had been a last resort, one he'd hoped would preserve his life, not shorten it.

Hell, he hadn't counted on losing. He'd been down five grand, a position in which he'd been dozens of times, but he'd always come back from there to win or at least break even. With the open cards on the table and Eli's hole cards, he'd had a straight flush to the queen, only beatable by a royal flush. The only way Diaz could have won was if his hole cards were the king and ace of diamonds. Odds of that were about one in half a million.

When the betting had reached ten thousand, Eli had been positive that Rodrigo was bluffing, just waiting for Eli to fold. The moment Rodrigo had laid down his cards, Eli had been sure that some unseen force had sucked all the oxygen out of the room. Diaz had let him leave the suite, telling him that he had until morning to pay up. How could Eli have known that the guy was so shady, or that he was such an early riser?

Rodrigo lit a cigarette and blew smoke directly at Eli. "Were you trying to stiff me? Tell me the truth. You have the fifteen large or not?"

Eli's throat closed up. He coughed. "Who can think with all this toxic smoke in the air?"

Sven opened a panel on the back side of the front seat, revealing a small bar. He grabbed a plastic water bottle from the well and twisted off the cap before handing it to Eli.

Rodrigo shrugged. "We have lots of ways to get you to answer."

After several sips, Eli's stomach threatened to

send the water back up. He drew a deep breath. "Is this a multiple choice test, or fill in the blank?"

"You're not as amusing as you think." Rodrigo raised a thick eyebrow. "And I'm not as patient as you seem to think."

Eli shuddered at Rodrigo's menacing scowl. "Can we work something out? I need some time, a month, maybe two, tops."

The four other men in the SUV laughed—not chuckles but big, hearty guffaws.

Eli's shoulders and neck knotted. "Okay, a few weeks then."

Rodrigo wiped ash off of his lapel. "How do you plan to raise the cash?"

No clue. After Eli's recent losing streak, he was too tapped out to even get himself into any card games. "I can contact some friends and relatives, see what I can come up with." In truth, he knew that no one would help him. Those wells had dried up long ago.

The backseat henchman's smirk told Eli he'd better come up with a more concrete idea and fast. Before Eli could think of anything, Rodrigo spoke. "Because this is my first dealing with you, and because I like you, I'm going to cut you a break."

The guy wasn't going to merely forgive such a big debt. Deafening silence settled in the SUV.

Finally, Rodrigo spoke. "Manny, give me the box."

The man in the front passenger seat handed Diaz a leather case the size of a hardcover book. Could be a small caliber pistol inside.

Eli set his hands on his knees to keep them from shaking.

The driver turned onto a deserted street lined with warehouses in every shade of gray. Several blocks down he parked the Escalade in a gloomy, desolate lot.

Eli's hope evaporated. What did they have planned? This would be a great spot to kill someone. Hot fear washed through him.

Rodrigo opened the leather case to reveal a very old-looking gold brooch with pins extending out from the left and right. The rounded square centerpiece was inlaid with emeralds and rubies. "Know what this is?"

Eli was just thankful that it wasn't a firearm. Meeting the older man's stare, he shook his head. Whatever the piece was, the fact that Rodrigo had chosen to show it to him wasn't good.

"This is a cloak pin that dates back to medieval times," Rodrigo explained. "It's part of my collection of antique amulets, and it belonged to a wealthy Scottish lord who lived hundreds of years ago. He had a matching one made for his wife. That one was a little different, though. It had a sapphire in the center—a very special sapphire, with a certain…power. That one was lost a long time ago." He snapped the box shut. "Since I'm in a good mood today, I'm not going to cut off your hand, which is what I would usually do when somebody attempts to stiff me. I subscribe to the biblical eye-for-an-eye method of justice."

Justice, huh? Eli gulped. His tongue stuck to the roof of his mouth.

"Instead you're going to do me a favor," Rodrigo continued. "You understand? Today's your lucky day."

He didn't feel particularly lucky. Pulse racing, Eli nodded mutely. Thank God they weren't going to kill him, at least not right at the moment.

Rodrigo ran a finger along the top of the leather case, a lot like someone might touch a lover's face. "I recently learned that the matching brooch surfaced at a gem show out west a few years ago. Unfortunately, a gemologist named Len Cartwright snapped it up and refused to consider my generous offers for it. He kicked off a couple months back and left it to his daughter. Apparently, she doesn't want to sell it either, so I have to resort to other means. Which is where you come in, my friend."

Eli didn't like the sound of this, but most anything would be better than a bullet to the head.

Sven handed Eli a flash drive.

"That's all the information we have on the young lady. You get that sapphire brooch from her and turn it over to me. And in return, I let you keep both your hands." Rodrigo gave him a smile that made Eli's blood run cold.

Head pounding, Eli shoved the flash drive in his pocket. "But if she's already refused to sell it…"

"Then you'll have to either convince her to part with it, or you'll steal it." He patted Eli's left hand. "Righty or lefty?"

The other men laughed.

"And don't take too long. Capiche?" Diaz snuffed out his cigarette in the ashtray.

Sven opened his door and climbed out.

"Your sister is very pretty, Mr. Kincaid." Rodrigo shook his head. "Such a shame about her illness."

The words sent a chill down Eli's spine. His

panic immediately morphed into anger. He fisted his hands. "Don't you dare go near her."

Sven yanked him out of the vehicle by his collar. "Watch your manners. Mr. Diaz is being exceedingly kind to you."

How had they found out about Lizzy? She didn't even share his last name.

"We'll be in touch." Rodrigo nodded to Sven, who then gave Eli a hard shove, reminding him of how badly his ribs hurt. Sven climbed back inside and shut the door.

The Escalade sped away.

Coughing through the cloud of dust, Eli reached into his pocket for the flash drive and closed his fingers around it.

He had no choice but to do what Diaz had asked. Hell, if he didn't, he'd lose an important body part. Worse, they could hurt Lizzy. A chill rolled over his skin. He couldn't let anything happen to her. She'd already suffered so much. He'd do whatever it took to protect her.

# Chapter One

Samantha Cartwright parked on Whiskers Lane, across the street from the quaint alcove that led to Eye of Newt Metaphysical Shop. She offered up a silent wish that this would be the fresh start she'd been hoping for. The old Impala sputtered and shuddered as she shut it off. Opening the car door, she inhaled the thick, salt-scented humidity. Even at nine-fifteen in the morning, the September heat had already reached unbearable. She'd missed it here—the beach, the boardwalk, the adorable cat-themed town. Home.

Excitement bubbled up inside her as she strode into Calico Court, the alleyway between two buildings, although being there was always bittersweet. The town was truly magical—a large proportion of the locals possessed some kind of supernatural gift. Since nearly all of Sam's female relatives were magically inclined, it stood to reason that Sam should also have some otherworldly power. Only she didn't. Being home reminded her of that deficit.

She heard the familiar, calming sound of the

fountain in the center of the space before she saw it. The three wrought iron bistro tables outside Medici restaurant held vases of orange and yellow blooms. She glanced into the window of The Zen Den, where a young woman Sam didn't recognize was teaching a yoga class to a small group. Next door, the red and white closed sign with a clock face set to ten o'clock hung in the window of her great-aunt's store, the same sign Aunt Emma had been using for as far back as Sam could remember.

Sam's mood clunked a little. She'd traveled a long way after her aunt's cryptic phone message, and now she had no choice but to wait a bit more until Emma opened.

But she took solace in the smell of coffee and fresh-baked pastries coming from the Cove Cat Café next door, so she headed over for one of the best lattes in town. After two days of driving, a cup of strong coffee and one of Luna's homemade cinnamon buns would hit the spot.

Digging into the pocket of her peasant dress, Sam pulled out a couple crinkled bills. Maybe she should get her sketchpad and pencils out of her car, but Luna might not want Sam to draw café customers for cash without prior permission. Better to just settle for coffee and skip the sweet. Aunt Emma always kept a stash of sugary snacks. As soon as her aunt arrived and opened the store, Sam would pilfer one of her favorite treats—a Moon Pie.

Walking around a purple bicycle parked outside the café, she pulled open the door and inhaled the aromas of cinnamon, chocolate, and maple. Sam's stomach growled in anticipation of an indulgence it wasn't destined to receive.

No sooner had she cleared the front door of the café when she spotted Luna's distinctive long, teal-colored braids. Luna slipped a still-steaming pie onto the upper shelf of the glass display next to the register.

Sam hung her bag over the back of a chair and went up to the counter, taking her place in line behind a grey-haired woman in a purple uniform. Sam realized the lady in front of her was none other than the town's cat officer—the person responsible for the care and feeding of the cats that resided on and around the grounds of the historic Sherwood house.

Little had changed at the café—the neon cat in the window, the colorful dreamcatchers hanging by the windows, the whirr of the cappuccino machine. Sam loved this place—part café, part cat rescue. Although Cove Cat Café had only been around for seven or eight years, it had been an almost overnight sensation, and now it was as much a part of the town as the clocktower in the middle of Wilshire Park and the historic Sherwood House with its formal gardens and free-roaming cats. She glanced through the large window that separated the cat rescue from the café. A pretty blonde wearing a black T-shirt with the café's logo was playing with the cats. Sam didn't recognize her, though.

"Be right with you," Luna said without looking at Sam.

"Take your time."

Luna stilled for a second before whipping her head around and fixing Sam with a wide-eyed stare. "Holy cow! You're here." She hurriedly closed the case and wiped her hands on the front of her black apron. Then she rounded the counter and pulled Sam into her arms, letting out an excited cheer. After a few seconds, she backed away to give Sam the once-over. "You look exhausted. What'd you sleep in your car or something?"

Sam rolled her eyes. "Sort of." Actually, she'd spent part of the night camped out at a state park off the interstate in Georgia, but when the mosquitos had started biting, she'd packed up and hit the road again.

"What can I get you?" Luna gestured toward the menu board on the wall.

"A latte and…" She'd figure out a way to earn some money. She always did. "How much are the cinnamon buns?"

"Four-twenty-five," Luna supplied.

Sam swallowed hard. "Um, okay." Aunt Emma had said in her message that the brooch Sam had recently inherited from her dad was the key to her future. Surely that future would include a better financial outlook.

Luna got to work on the latte. She set the coffee and cinnamon bun on a small tray and handed it to Sam. "You're too skinny. Consider this my contribution to putting some meat on your bones."

"You're the best, Luna." Sam's stomach seconded the sentiment with a rumble.

Luna waved off Sam's thanks. "Don't think I'm not upset with you for staying away so long. Four years without a visit is unforgivable."

Sam straightened, suddenly feeling like the awkward seventeen-year-old she'd been last time she'd seen Luna. "Sorry about that." Sam had been determined to make it on her own, without Aunt Emma's help. In the years since she'd left the town, though, she'd barely made ends meet.

The door opened, and several customers walked in.

"You're not off the hook until we have a proper sit-down conversation," Luna said. "I'm shorthanded this morning, and I've got to get back to work, but Emma left something for you." She reached under the counter and handed Sam a white envelope with her name on it in her aunt's almost-illegible handwriting.

What did Aunt Emma have to tell her that couldn't wait until the shop opened? Whatever it was would have to keep until after Sam got something in her stomach. After she sat down, she bit into the cinnamon bun and shut her eyes for a moment, savoring the gooey brown sugar and cinnamon, the sprinkling of chopped pecans, and the warm dough.

"Hey, sweet pea," a woman said with a thick, southern drawl.

Sam peered over her shoulder a moment before Ramona wrapped her in a hug.

"Hi. How are you?" Sam asked the hairdresser as she stood up.

A serene smile lit up Ramona's round face. "Never better." She held her hand up for Sam to see the diamond on her ring finger then fluffed her bleached-blond hair. "Engaged to the best guy in the world." Ramona lowered her voice. "A man of magic, and I'm not just talkin' about his bedroom skills." She waggled her eyebrows.

Sam snickered at Ramona's comment, although she couldn't imagine how anyone would willingly consent to be tied to another person for the rest of her life. Even if that man *was* magic. Guys came and went. Not a one could be trusted to stick around. She had to admit though, she was envious of anyone who had supernatural powers since Sam had been unlucky enough to not inherit any of the magical gifts that her maternal relatives all seemed to possess. "That's...great, I guess."

Ramona frowned. "You guess?"

Sam mentally smacked herself. "No, I didn't mean it like... Just forget it. Congrats. I wish you the best."

Ramona squeezed Sam's arm. "Come on over to the salon later, and I'll give you a trim—on the house. No offense, but you need it, hon. Can't wait to hear what you've been up to. Setting the art world on fire by now, no doubt."

"No fires yet, but thanks for the vote of confidence. I might take you up on that offer, though."

"Please do. I'll fill you in on all the gossip. Ooh! You should get a reading from our new nail tech, Mallory. She's really good." Ramona slapped a hand over her mouth. "What am I thinking? Your Aunt Emma does great readings, too."

Sam nodded. "She does." A reading was a great idea, actually. Sam would ask her aunt after they caught up. She certainly had a lot of questions about her future. Maybe Aunt Emma's advice would help Sam figure out what she should be doing and how she could make enough money to get by on her own.

By far, the most pressing question she had was whether to sell the sapphire brooch. Certainly, she needed the money. Her aunt's message had been clear about one thing—Sam wasn't to do anything with the jewel, at least until after she and Emma had an in-person talk.

The antique sapphire pin was pretty big, and no doubt worth a hefty chunk of change, but the stone's value went beyond its actual monetary worth. According to Sam's dad, the jewel had magical properties. When someone held it or wore it, lying was impossible for them. So many people had been dishonest with Sam. If what her dad had said was for real, she could easily figure out when someone was telling the truth, and when they weren't, merely by handing them the stone and asking them a question. That knowledge could come in handy, especially since people had lied to Sam her whole life. And in truth, maybe owning a magical piece of jewelry was the next best thing to actually having the gift of magic. Yet, if she sold the sapphire, she could afford to rent space in a gallery for her work.

A lawyer had contacted Sam right after her father's death last month, telling her he had a client interested in the jewel. She hadn't been ready to part with the only thing she had of her dad, even though the lawyer had insisted his client was prepared to make her a generous offer. When she'd turned him down, he'd given her his number and insisted that whenever she was ready, his buyer was interested.

Sam pulled out her aunt's handwritten letter. Emma had filled up the entire page with her tiny, messy cursive writing. Sam deciphered as much as she could: Her aunt needed her to work the store for the next ten days. *What?* Was there something wrong with Aunt Emma? Was she ill? Sam's mouth was suddenly dry as charcoal. She continued reading.

*"I can't explain now why I can't be there, but as soon as I return, we'll have a lovely visit,"* Emma wrote. She went on to tell Sam that she'd prepared her old room

in the house and that she'd stocked the fridge with some of Sam's favorites—spaghetti casserole, Scotch eggs, and a rhubarb pie.

The rest of the letter was detailed instructions for taking care of Emma's cat, Ginger—when and what to feed her, where her toys were kept, and how often to brush her.

But there was almost no information about working the store. How was Sam supposed to run a business she hadn't even entered in years? Sure, she'd helped out there on weekends and summer vacation when she was a teenager, but Emma had always been there, overseeing everything. What if she screwed it up? She hardly knew anything about the essential oils, crystals, and other spiritual items her aunt carried.

Perhaps a reading would tell her if she was up to the challenge.

Sam ate the rest of her cinnamon bun while she waited for Ramona to finish paying for her coffee and pastry. When Ramona strode to the condiment station, Sam grabbed her coffee cup and joined her. "Do you think I could get a reading now?"

Ramona dumped three sugar packets into her coffee. "I'm sure someone could squeeze you in. Come on."

Sam waved to Luna. "I'll be back later," she told the barista.

"You'd better." Luna threw her a wink.

Sam followed Ramona next door to Claws-N-Coifs. The heavy odors of hairspray and nail polish permeated the air. The décor was still the same pink and black as Sam remembered, with four hair stations lining one wall, three nail tables on the other side, and a tall reception desk in the waiting area near the door.

Two hairdressers were working on clients.

Ramona set her coffee and pastry down at her station then strode toward the two manicurists. "Hey, y'all. Anybody got time to give my friend Sam here a reading?"

"I can do it as soon as I finish with Ms. Watson's manicure," a pretty blonde told Ramona.

Sam nodded at the nail tech. Why did she look so familiar? Then it hit her. Sam had just seen her at the cat café, but she'd been wearing a black T-shirt with the café's logo. Now she had on a cute red and white polka dot dress. Sam nudged Ramona. "I-I'm confused."

Ramona widened her eyes at Sam. "What's wrong, doll?"

Sam tipped her chin toward the blonde manicurist. "I swear I just saw that woman at the café."

"Hmm. Maybe you're coming down with something." Ramona touched her hand to Sam's forehead. Then she burst out laughing. "Sorry, sweet pea. I'm messing with you. Mallory here has a twin. Jordan works at the cat rescue next door."

Sam grinned. "You're rotten, Ramona."

"You have no idea, doll." Hooking Sam's arm, the hairdresser led her to the sofa. "Mallory's our newest nail tech. And she'll give you a good reading, too." Ramona pointed at Sam's hands. "Those paws of yours could use some pampering."

"We'll see. Thanks, Ramona." Sam sat down in the waiting area and folded her hands in her lap. She'd given up on trying to keep up her fingernails. With all the painting she did, her skin was permanently pigmented purple.

Minutes later, Mallory came over. "You wanted a reading?"

Sam stood. "How much is it?"

"I gather you're a friend of Ramona's. I'll give you the friends and family discount. How does ten bucks sound?"

Like all Sam could afford at the moment. "That's fine. Thanks."

Mallory led Sam to her nail table and sat across from her. She handed Sam a deck of tarot cards. "Shuffle them and think about what you'd like them to tell you."

Where to begin? So many things in her life were in a state of flux—her career, her living arrangements, her finances, her aunt's whereabouts. But she couldn't expect Mallory to portent every aspect of her life. So she concentrated on the sapphire brooch. She finished mixing the deck and set it on the table. "I need to know what I should do with…something that I recently…acquired."

"Okay." Mallory fanned out the deck. "Pick three."

When she did, Mallory studied the cards for several moments before tapping one that depicted a man and woman dancing under the moon. "The moon. Could mean a whirlwind romance."

Sam laughed. "Not likely."

Shrugging, Mallory continued. "The relationship portended here would be powerful, almost intoxicating, but it isn't one you can trust." She pointed to the next card. "A man who might mean you harm."

Sam knew better than to trust in any relationship, which was why she planned to avoid them for the foreseeable future. "What about my question? The item I asked about."

Mallory looked at each card in turn. "That decision isn't in your hands."

Sam narrowed her eyes at the psychic. "But it belongs to me. Of course, it's my decision."

Mallory shook her head. "Not right now it isn't, but that could change. I'm just telling you what the cards say." She pointed to the deck. "Think about what you desire most then pick one more card."

Sam concentrated on her future. Would she ever find success as an artist? What did she have to do in order to achieve her dreams? She drew a card and handed it to Mallory.

The blonde widened her eyes as she laid the card on the table. "Very interesting. This one is all about visions and illusions, and even creative arts."

Sam sat up taller.

"It can be a warning about hidden enemies," Mallory said. "But it also portents amazing creativity and powerful magic."

"Magic?" Sam's pulse raced.

"Mm-hmm. Be warned, though. You might be facing a time of emotional and mental trial. Your mind could play tricks on you. Try to keep your senses about you. Don't let that whirlwind romance knock you off balance."

Fat chance. And magic? Not likely. So much for Mallory's fortune-telling abilities.

Maybe when Aunt Emma returned, Sam would get a more accurate reading from her. All her life, Sam had wished for some sort of magical gift—like Aunt Emma's psychic ability, Sam's mother's gift of clairaudience, or Grandma Selma's power to move objects with her mind. But the spring of supernatural talents that ran through so much of her family had apparently made a detour around Sam.

Rather than dispute the reader's claim, Sam merely shrugged and passed her aunt's letter across the table. "What do you make of this?"

Mallory quickly scanned the note then held it between her hands before giving it back to Sam. "I'm not picking up any weird vibes from the letter. What is it you want to know?"

"What's going on with my Aunt Emma. She didn't say a word about going out of town. It's unlike her to be so…secretive."

"Oh, you're talking about Emma from Eye of Newt. I saw her last week. She said she was going on a cruise."

"A cruise?" Sam's heart sank. Emma would be totally incommunicado until she came home. Sam would have to wait so long to find out what her aunt's message about the sapphire meant.

Mallory furrowed her brow. "The vacation will do her good. She works all the time. Is that what you're worried about? That she's sick or something? I can see your point. A vacation is out of character for her. I'm sure Emma's fine, though."

Exhaling a little of her tension, Sam smiled. "Yeah, that was it. I guess I'm no good at putting my questions into words."

"Nothing else I can answer for you?"

Sam considered that. "Would you happen to know how I'm supposed to get into the store?"

"Luna has the key. The PS on the back of the letter said so."

How had Sam missed that? "Okay, thanks."

She set two crinkled five-dollar bills on Mallory's table. "I guess I'll be seeing you around."

"Hope so. It was nice to meet you." Sam returned to the café.

Luna waved her past the line of customers. "You just want a refill?"

"Definitely." Sam set her cup on the counter. "Did my aunt leave a key here for me?"

Luna smacked her forehead. "Sorry. I completely forgot." She handed Sam a fresh latte and a ring with two keys. "She said one is for the store and the other is to the cottage."

"Thanks, Luna. I'll see you later." Picking up her coffee, she turned to leave and crashed into a man. Somehow, the paper cup smashed between them, spilling hot coffee all over both of them. "Oh, God. I'm so sorry." She grabbed a stack of napkins from the counter and handed them to the best-looking guy with the greenest eyes she'd ever seen, like viridian paint with a smidge of gold mixed in. And damn, did he smell great. His cologne reminded her of the crisp, clean scent of the beach when her mom's carnival had done stints in Wildwood, New Jersey, or Ocean City, Maryland.

"I'm not." Giving her a wink, he grinned. "Well, I am sorry for causing you to spill your drink all over yourself."

A zing of heat skittered through her as he patted his shirt and jacket with the napkins. "N-no, it was my fault. I should have looked where I was going." She reached for more napkins to clean herself up. Geez, he was ridiculously handsome, like someone you'd see on a billboard ad for men's cologne or on the cover of a sexy romance novel.

But she wasn't interested in any guy, let alone a suit kind of guy. Totally not her type. Hell, she'd had enough of hot men in pricey suits after spending a few weeks working on a mural at a high-end men's clothing store in New York. One, in particular, had relentlessly flirted with her until she'd gone out with him. After he'd wined and dined her, she'd gone home with him for a weekend of passion, followed by him unceremoniously dumping her.

Nope, she definitely wanted no part of a guy like him. She cleared her throat. "I should go clean up." Without waiting for the man's response, she hurried to the restroom.

A little soap and cold water later, she was still damp, but clean. Hopefully, the hot guy was gone by now. She left the bathroom then went to apologize to Luna for the mess she'd made.

"No prob," Luna said. She handed Sam a bag. "It's a chocolate croissant."

Sam shook her head. "You don't have to—"

"Wasn't me," Luna said. "The cutie in Brooks Brothers bought it for you and gave me a generous tip. Paying it forward or something, huh?"

Sam glanced at the door in time to catch a quick glimpse of the suit guy leaving. "That was nice of him."

Luna nodded. "Good luck running the store, kiddo."

"Thanks." She'd need it. Minutes later, when she unlocked the door of Eye of Newt and stepped inside, memories bombarded her, both bitter and sweet. As a small child, she'd played jacks on the wide-plank oak floor. More than once, her mother had dumped her with Aunt Emma for months or years on end. How many evenings had she spent drawing at the round table in the back room while Emma worked?

Three narrow shelves stretched the entire length of one wall, each packed with large glass jars of neatly labeled herbs and teas. The large apothecary cabinet near the picture window was new, but she was pretty sure that, like the old one had, it held a vast selection of small bottles of essential oils—tea tree, lime, orange, rose.

The long L-shaped glass display counter held tons of her aunt's handmade earrings, bracelets, rings, and necklaces on one side, and various items relating to the herbs and oils on the other—aroma diffusers, packs of charcoal, sensors, and incense burners.

She stashed her bag under the counter, flipped over the open sign, and turned on the lights.

How in the world was she going to manage running the business for the next ten days? And since when did Emma take vacations? Why hadn't she told Sam she'd be away? Now she'd have to wait more than a week to get all the details about her aunt's message and learn why she was so insistent that Sam hold onto the sapphire.

Before she could dwell on her dilemma, two customers walked in—an elderly woman, and a younger redheaded one—and started browsing. Sam gave them a cursory nod as she searched for the power button on the electronic cash register.

"Where's the mugwort?" the senior asked her. "And I need ylang-ylang oil, too."

Sam checked the apothecary drawers for labels that started with L. After a minute she gave up. "We might not have that."

Huffing, the customer pointed her cane toward the far end of the cabinet. "It starts with a Y. Would you give me a quarter-ounce bottle?"

The younger woman approached Sam. "What's good for relaxation?" she asked. "I've been having so much trouble sleeping lately."

A headache stabbed behind Sam's eyes. She wiped a bead of sweat from her brow. If only she'd taken an interest in her aunt's inventory when she'd lived with her.

Sam rubbed her temples. "I'll be right with you, ma'am." As Sam fished in the cabinet for the oils the older woman wanted, the door chimed again. Yikes. How did Aunt Emma expect Sam to handle this? And why wasn't there any mugwort in the M drawer?

The lady looked at Sam as if she was a complete idiot, an expression she was all too familiar with. "Mugwort herb, not oil," the woman said.

From behind them, a man cleared his throat. "Did someone say mugwort?"

Sam glanced over her shoulder at him and realized that he was the guy who'd paid her tab at the café, the man she'd spilled her coffee on.

He retrieved a glass jar from the highest shelf.

"Thank you," she said.

One corner of his mouth lifted in a subtle grin as he set the jar down next to the register.

Had he followed her? He was too handsome and well-dressed to be a weirdo or a stalker. Not that she'd personally known any of either variety. Heck, criminals could be handsome, couldn't they? She'd seen a story on the news about a man out west who got a modeling contract based on his jail booking photo.

Slipping behind the counter, she covertly opened the drawer where Emma had always kept a knife. When she glimpsed a flash of silver from the drawer, she drew a relieved breath; although she was ninety-nine percent sure the man was harmless.

The customer set her purse on the counter and fished out her wallet. "I don't have all day, miss."

"Yes, ma'am." Sam keyed in the prices on the cash register. "That'll be nine-sixty."

The woman handed her a ten. "I don't have my glasses with me. Would you please read me the back of the label on the essential oil bottle? I want to be sure I'm getting the right one."

Sam held the tiny bottle close to her face and read the tiny print. "Sweet, floral ylang-ylang is a natural aphrodisiac."

Hot guy waggled his eyebrows at the older woman, but luckily she was checking out the jewelry in the display. When he met Sam's stare, amusement shone in his eyes.

Sam held back a chuckle and continued reading the label. "Use in aromatherapy to relieve anxiety and tension. Associated with the heart chakra. Helps to bring emotional balance and self-love."

"Sound like great stuff," the man said. His grin widened when he shifted his gaze to Sam. "No aphrodisiac needed for me."

Warmth rose in her cheeks.

"Smells nice, too," the woman said.

Sam packed the customer's purchases in a bag along with her receipt and handed it to her. "Have a good day."

"Can you direct me to the best essential oils

for relaxation?" the redhead asked Sam.

"Um, sure," Sam replied. Did Aunt Emma have a cheat sheet somewhere? A guide to what herbs and oils were for? A quick search behind the counter didn't turn up anything helpful.

"Lavender is supposed to be good for that," hot guy offered. "And chamomile. Together, they'll knock out even the most hyper person."

The redhead closed the distance the man and gave him a sultry grin that made Sam's gut clench. Which was totally ridiculous. Sam wouldn't give a hoot if every woman in town flirted with him. Why should she? She had no interest in him. Zero.

"I'm glad someone here is knowledgeable," the young woman stage-whispered to the man. "This isn't the only metaphysical shop in town, after all."

To his credit, hot guy ignored the woman's comment. She shrugged then headed to the herb section.

Sam threw the man a grateful smile.

"I'll take these." The redhead set two bags of herbs on the counter.

Sam rang her up and tried for a polite—if not warm—thank you. "Come back and see us."

The woman rolled her eyes as she took her bag.

The moment the lady was out the door, the man turned to Sam. "I've finally gotten you alone."

Was he just flirting with her? Or were his intentions sinister?

# Chapter Two

What the hell was wrong with him? Worst thing he could do was to frighten or embarrass the poor woman. Bad enough that he was going to have to steal from her. He needed to gain her trust, and fast, yet she was backing away from him, blinking like a terrified child. She escaped behind the counter, her expression stiff and guarded.

He tried his best, most charming smile, but she didn't budge.

Her throat twitched with a swallow, and he couldn't help but notice her long, lovely neck. She folded her arms over her chest. "What do you mean by that?"

He'd planned to quickly gain her trust, find out where she had the brooch then disappear from her life. Unfortunately, she wasn't going to be the pushover he'd hoped. He knew way more than he should about Samantha Cartwright. Although certain things hadn't been included in the file he'd been given, he'd quickly ascertained that she had little self-confidence. Which baffled him, because not only was she a talented artist, but she was also so much prettier than her photo. With her thick mass of long auburn waves and the fire in her deep blue eyes, he couldn't believe that she didn't have a boyfriend or husband lurking about.

Raising his arms in surrender, he took a backward step to set her at ease. "Sorry. I didn't mean to scare you or come on too strong. It's just that…the moment we crashed into each other at the café, I felt an instant connection with you. I was hoping you had, too." When she didn't say anything, he continued. "I'm Eli. And apparently, I suck at reading signals."

She held her ground…and her tongue.

He had to wonder if the information he had on her was valid. In a floral-pattern peasant dress, five-dollar sandals, and a bunch of cheap bangles and beaded bracelets on each wrist, she hardly appeared the kind of woman who'd turn down an opportunity to sell a valuable gem. He'd never been a fan of the bohemian look, but on her, it worked. There was no denying that she was gorgeous, nor that she was completely unaware of her beauty. The only makeup she wore was a little pink lip-gloss. Her features didn't need any enhancement. Her skin was peaches and cream fresh, and those long eyelashes showed off her eyes better than the war paint most women wore. After two days of following her, he'd only seen her from afar, until a little while ago. This close to her, he could appreciate the sprinkling of freckles across her cheeks and the way her hair shone in the light.

No, he refused to let a pretty face distract him from his mission. Going town to town—Las Vegas, Reno, Atlantic City—he'd seen his share of beauties. One- or two-night stands were his MO. Sam was the antithesis of the type of woman with whom he kept company. He'd always gone for Park Avenue rather than Greenwich Village. Besides, he planned to get the heck out of dodge the moment he got his hands on that sapphire brooch. The sooner he had the trinket and delivered it to Diaz, the sooner he and his sister would be safe.

"Honestly, I just came over here to offer to pay for your dress since I ruined it." He swept a hand through the air. "You looked pretty overwhelmed when I came in here so I figured I could be of help."

Her flinch was subtle. Picking up on such things was how he'd been able to make a living at card games. Well, until recently, when a string of bad luck had culminated in that high-stakes poker game where he'd been dead wrong about Diaz's hand. If only he could go back and replay it. But he couldn't. All he could do now was capitulate. Diaz had made that abundantly clear. If he failed, the shark's henchmen would do a lot worse than break Eli's ribs as they had a few days ago. There was no way he'd put his sister in danger. Lizzy had been through enough.

Unfortunately, Eli was way out of his element. He was a gambler, after all, not a criminal. As soon as he completed the task Diaz had given him, though, a bona fide criminal was exactly what he'd be. Lizzy would be so disappointed in him if she ever found out. She'd given him a college education in hopes that he'd stay on the straight and narrow, something she hadn't been able to do. But the working-stiff life hadn't appealed to him.

Illegal activities had never been his thing, though—nothing more than poker tournaments and the occasional private, high-stakes game. Until now. He had no choice but to do the job because he couldn't afford the consequences. Period.

"Someone will be here soon to help me." Sam squared her shoulders but lowered her gaze. He'd seen similar contradictory body language more than once at gaming tables. "My…boyfriend, Big Bruno," she said.

Eli held back a laugh at her bluff. She was a lousy liar, but the fact that she'd felt the need to conjure up an imaginary boyfriend confirmed that she was leery of him. And for good reason. "Big Bruno," he repeated. "Sounds like a scary guy. I'd hate for him to get the wrong impression about us."

"And what would that be?" She bit her lip.

"That there's some chemistry bouncing around between us." He gave her his most charming grin.

A rosy flush crawled up her neck, and settled on her cheeks. "I don't think so."

Shrugging, he gave the store a final glance. "My bad. Guess I should leave before he gets here."

"Probably. He's very protective of me."

Starting toward the door, he stuck his hand in his jacket pocket and fingered his good luck poker chip, the very first he'd won. He wasn't ready to fold yet.

"Thanks for the croissant," she said.

Her words gave him a modicum of hope that the story he'd made up had worked. But she wasn't sold yet. Without facing her, he waved. "Don't mention it."

*Three, two, one…*

"Hey," she called. "I'm Samantha. Sam."

“Have a nice life, Samantha,” he said over his shoulder as he grasped the doorknob.

“I didn’t mean to be rude.” She sighed. “I’m not used to people doing nice things for me.”

Turning around, he glimpsed the vulnerability in her expression. Shouldn’t bother him, but it did. He dropped her gaze for a moment. “Then you deserve to be treated better.” A lot better than the way he planned to do her.

She shook her head. “Not really.”

His gut clenched.

*I have to do this.*

A middle-aged couple came in, followed by two young women.

Sam slipped behind the counter and rubbed the bridge of her nose.

Eli returned to the counter and kept his voice low. “You know, I don’t mind helping you here for a little while.”

Her expression registered interest for a moment. Too quickly, she frowned. “I can’t ask you to do that. We don’t even know each other.”

The opportunity to get close to her was like a neon sign beckoning him to go for it, and not only because he needed that sapphire. In truth, he’d been drawn to her from the moment he’d seen her through his binoculars. Her earthy attractiveness was so unusual, so sensual. He didn’t want to have to steal from her, but what choice did he have?

She’d eventually get over the loss. If he didn’t do what Rodrigo Diaz wanted him to, the son of a bitch would surely follow through on his threat to cut off Eli’s hand, and maybe even go after Lizzy. No way could he put his sister in that bastard’s crosshairs.

He'd already let Lizzy down enough.

Squashing the stab of guilt jabbing his insides, he waved off Sam's objections. "How can you say we don't know each other? We shared a cup of coffee, did our laundry together." He winked at her. "Sort of."

That earned him a chuckle, but before she could say anything, the door chime rang, and a young brunette came in. She glanced around for a few seconds, then peered toward the back of the store. "Is Emma doing a reading?"

Sam shook her head. "She's not here. Can I help you?"

The brunette pursed her lips, pulled a crinkled piece of paper out of her purse, and handed it to Sam. "I need all those items. Except for the sandalwood oil. I've got that."

Sam furrowed her brow as she stared at the paper, but Eli didn't offer his assistance. Better to give her time to realize how much she needed him. When her gaze drifted to him, he was sure she was about to fold. Until she touched her finger to the sheet. "White sage," she read. "That should be on the bottom shelf." She went to get it.

"One of the large bundles," the customer said. "I just moved, and I need to smudge my new place."

Sam smiled at her, clearly a little relieved. Until she returned her attention to the woman's list. Her throat twitched with a swallow. "Um, let's see—lavender, feverfew, diatomaceous earth …"

"Miss," a male customer called to Sam. Do you have any polished shungite?"

Sam blinked several times, which was one of

her tells. Clearly, she was overwhelmed. "I-I'm not sure."

Unable to bear Sam's discomfort another second, Eli covertly checked the other customer's list. "Want me to get the lavender and the feverfew down for you?"

Sam gave him a slight nod. "I'd appreciate that."

Reaching to a high shelf for the purple buds, his sore ribs reminded him of his mission. "I'll get the diatomaceous earth, Sam. I see it up on the top shelf."

"Thank you." While she fetched the crystal for the woman, Eli rechecked the customer's list and rounded up the other items.

Sam rang up both orders, and Eli bagged them.

After the customers left, Sam exhaled loudly. "Wow, thank you so much. I don't know what I would have done without you."

His gut tightened as he shrugged off her gratitude. "How are you going to manage here for the rest of the day? Well, assuming that *Big Bruno* doesn't show."

Another blush bloomed on her cheeks. "I kind of…made that up."

Chuckling, he took a few steps toward her. "Really? I'd have never guessed." He grabbed his phone out of his pocket and opened the calendar app for effect. "I have some time now. I could stay for a while."

Her pretty eyes brightened and the wariness that had been there earlier vanished. "You'd do that?"

It was the least he could do, considering he planned to rob her of the brooch and hand it over to

Diaz. "Let's just say that someone did me a solid once. I don't mind at all."

In truth, no one had ever done anything kind for him, not without expectations. Well, except for Lizzy. Which was why he couldn't let her down, or let her find out how far he'd fallen.

He had to get that jewel. Yet looking into Sam's innocent eyes, part of him wished that she'd throw him out, tell him to take his bogus offer of assistance and shove it. The other part of him wanted her to trust him—the side that knew Diaz didn't make empty threats.

She wrapped her arms around her body. "No. Absolutely not. I refuse to take up your time. Besides, I don't think this place gets very busy except when there's some big event in town, and those are usually on weekends. I'm sure all those customers at once was just a fluke. Most days, only a few customers come in. Unless business has picked up since I left several years ago."

On cue, a young couple entered the store, followed by a group of three women who appeared to be in their sixties. Despite Sam's insistence that she could handle it, clearly, she'd have a tough time.

"How about I just help get you through this rush?" he offered.

She caught her bottom lip between her teeth. After a short hesitation, she gave Eli a half nod—all the encouragement he needed.

Another customer came in looking for help with insomnia. "What herbs do you recommend?" she asked Sam.

Sam scratched her head. "Um, hang on a sec."

Eli reached for a book of herbal remedies

from among the small collection for sale. He thumbed through it until he found a chart of natural remedies and quickly scanned it. "Lavender near your bed should help. Also valerian capsules and California poppy." After gathering the items for the woman, he talked her into the book as well.

Sam grinned at him and started ringing up the sale. "Thank you," she mouthed.

He made the young couple a custom blend of lavender, rose, and ylang-ylang essential oils to use in a diffuser for their dog's anxiety.

Sam sniffed the concoction before wrapping it up. "Smells great."

"Emma made us a mix for stress," the man said. "It helped. So we figured why not try something similar for Ruff?"

That furrow on Sam's brow that he'd noticed earlier was gone.

More shoppers came and went. With him aiding the customers in scoping out various items, and Sam handling the transactions, they found their rhythm as if they'd been working together for years. He wished he was merely helping her out for its own sake, but her appreciative smiles and glances only served to poke at his conscience.

A couple hours after Sam had opened, the traffic finally slowed down. She sat on a stool behind the counter and leaned her chin on her hand. "That was kind of exhausting. I had no idea Aunt Emma's business had grown so much. She's been doing this for so long that it's second nature to her. I wish it weren't Greek to me."

Eli rubbed his hands together. "I think you're just warming up."

She rolled her eyes. "Scary thought. How about I close up for an hour for lunch and get you something to eat? My aunt won't mind buying us a meal. We've definitely earned that."

The opportunity to break bread with her was too good to pass up. The faster she started trusting him, the sooner he could find out where she kept the sapphire. He checked his phone. "It's almost two-thirty, way past lunchtime. But I never turn down a free meal or a beautiful woman."

Color flared in her cheeks again. She averted her gaze. "We could go back to the cat café. Or somewhere else."

Apparently, she knew some of the staff next door, but he wanted her all to himself. "I'm more of a meat eater, and they don't serve much besides croissants and pastries at the café."

She grabbed her bag from behind the counter and a twenty out of the register. "Fine with me. Purry's has amazing burgers." Before they left, she set the little clock on the closed sign to three-thirty.

Minutes later, they sat at a booth in the back corner of the diner. The jukebox played a familiar song from the sixties, but at the off-hour, hardly anyone was there to hear it. He took two menus from the stand on the table and handed one to Sam. A waitress in a pink uniform—who was seventy-five if she was a day—brought them water. "What'll it be, folks?"

"I'll have a cheeseburger and fries. And a Tuxedo milkshake." Sam returned her menu to the stand without ever opening it.

"Double that," Eli said.

After the waitress had retreated, Sam opened

her bag and took out a large spiral-bound tablet. "When I was a teenager, I used to hang out here and draw while Aunt Emma was at work." A sheepish grin settled on her lips. "I was supposed to be doing my homework. I was never much good at that."

"You didn't like school?"

"Wasn't that. I didn't have the brains for it, especially math and science." Her lips flattened to a thin line. "My mom always said I was stupid."

Eli's chest constricted. "I'm sure that's not true." How could any parent say such a thing to their child? His mother had been mostly absent from his life, so Lizzy had raised him in a stern yet loving manner. She always told him he could do anything he set his mind to. "You know, artistic people are more right-brained. People who are good at math and the sciences are left-brained."

The waitress dropped off their milkshakes, which were brown on one side and white on the other.

Sam pushed a straw into hers. "I doubt my mother would believe that. She just blamed my poor grades on my inferior intelligence."

He set his hand over hers, but she immediately withdrew from his touch.

"I'm sorry," he said. "That was…too forward of me." What was it about her that moved something deep inside him, a place he normally kept well-guarded? If he let Sam get under his skin, his job here would be so much more difficult. He tipped his chin at her sketch pad. "May I?"

"No." Sam tucked her hair behind her ears. "I'll show you a couple of my drawings." She flipped to the middle of the tablet. "My sketch pad is a lot like a diary. It's very personal." Turning the paper toward him, she said, "I did this one at a park along the interstate, somewhere in South Carolina, I think."

The charcoal drawing showed a young couple and two toddlers at a picnic table. Sam had managed to capture the warmth of the family moment.

She flipped to another page, a sketch of an elderly man walking with a child on a beach. "This is another one from my trip down here."

The frailty of the subject was palpable. As she showed him more, he could hardly believe his eyes. They were doodles really, but incredibly well-done pictures of people, a scene from a market, another of a house and garden. Eli didn't know much about art, but clearly, Sam had a lot of talent. "They're very good."

She rubbed the bridge of her nose. "Not good enough. I mean, I get by. I paint murals and portraits. It's tough to find commissions, though. My best work is in my portfolio." She closed the tablet. "Sometimes I redo the ones I jot down here on a larger scale, like the farmhouse. I painted a mural of that at a farmers' market in Virginia. Earned enough from that job to pay for new tires on my car, and gas for the trip down here."

If she was so hard up for money why didn't she just sell the sapphire? "Is that where you're from?" His information on her only went back two years.

Their food arrived, and she waited until the waitress left before speaking. "I'm from all over. My mom traveled with a carnival, working a few different arcade booths. I guess she still does that. Haven't heard from her for a few years." She ate a French fry.

He took a bite of his burger and waited for her to say more.

"Every time my mother went into rehab, I got to stay with my Aunt Emma. When I was twelve, my aunt told Mom that she was going to raise me. My mother didn't argue. She'd never wanted me anyway."

Eli clenched his jaw against a rush of empathy.

"I left here when I was seventeen to become a starving artist," Sam went on.

He'd have preferred not to learn how rough Sam's childhood had been. It only made his mission more difficult to reconcile. "I've lived a lot of places, too." At least that was true. He and Lizzy had moved a dozen times, although she'd never explained why. Eli had always had his suspicions. He'd seen bruises on Lizzy more than once, figured her clients sometimes got rough with her. His appetite all but dried up. He set his burger down.

Sam twisted her napkin. "When I was growing up, all I wanted was to be from somewhere, a hometown. There were a couple places the carnival went that I liked. I'd walk around town looking through windows of the homes, and I saw families spending time together, and I'd pretend this or that house was where I lived. In my head, I'd fill in the blanks—what my room looked like, and my parents, a little brother or sister. They were so lucky to have a home that wasn't on wheels, one that couldn't be moved."

Emotion thickened his throat. "So you quit school at seventeen?"

"Wasn't as if I was passing anyway. I finally decided to drop out during my junior year. I thought

Aunt Emma was going to kill me." She shrugged. "One day, I'll get my GED."

"How'd you end up in Virginia?"

Squeezing ketchup over her fries, she shook her head. "I was in upstate New York over the summer, selling my paintings and sketches to tourists in an artsy little town, until the weather cooled down and the crowds shrank down to almost nothing. After that, I headed south and managed to get the mural gig in Virginia. I was only there for a month."

Virginia was where Rodrigo had told him to find her, which meant the loan shark had had someone following her. Maybe he still did. Swallowing hard, Eli quickly scanned the restaurant. No one looked especially suspicious. If Rodrigo were that determined to get his hands on her sapphire, one way or another he would. And if Eli didn't manage to find the jewel, the next guy Rodrigo sent might hurt her, or worse. An ache stabbed behind his eyes.

Sam took a sip of her milkshake. "What about you? Do you live here?"

He probably should've come up with a cover story, but he hadn't anticipated the question. Another reason he was a lousy criminal. "Just temporarily." Technically true. Before she started probing more, he steered the topic back to her. "Do you plan to stay in town long?"

"Not sure yet." She reached for her burger and took a bite.

"We're just a couple of drifters, hmm?" In his case, more like a grafter.

Drawing her out wasn't as easy as he'd anticipated. Knowing as much as he could about his opponents had usually proved advantageous in card games. He didn't want to regard Sam as an opponent, though. He had to do this, had to get Sam to trust him. One thing was already clear—she had a healthy appetite for someone so thin. He'd glimpsed how frugal she'd been on her trip—sleeping in her car, eating at truck stops along the way, so maybe she'd just lost weight because she was too broke to eat well.

God, he despised Rodrigo for forcing him to do this to Sam.

"Do you have family in Cat's Paw Cove?" Sam asked.

An image of Lizzy in her wheelchair flashed in his mind—helpless, vulnerable. All because of him. "Um, no."

"What brought you here?"

Taking a sip of his milkshake to buy himself a moment, he thought about how to answer. "Work, actually."

"What do you do?" she asked.

"I'm an actor in a bad play," he deadpanned.

Sam huffed. "Come on."

"Okay, I'm a consultant." When he was a kid, he'd heard Lizzy tell people that was what she did—people from whom she wanted to hide the truth, like Eli's teachers, and social workers.

Sam narrowed her eyes at him for a moment before returning to her meal.

"How'd you learn to draw so well?" he asked.

"I'm self-taught."

"Are other members of your family gifted, too?"

A wry grin lifted one corner of her lips. "My relatives have other gifts, but not artistic ones."

He wondered what she'd meant by that.

"Sam Cartwright!" a woman squealed.

Sam waved to someone behind him but didn't appear to be particularly excited to see the other woman. "How are you, Alison?"

An attractive blonde approached their table and gave Sam a quick hug. "It's been ages, hasn't it?"

Sam smiled tightly. "Sure has."

The blonde slid her gaze to Eli and batted her eyelashes. "Well, hello there, handsome."

Eli ignored her come-on, turning his attention to his meal instead.

The woman took Sam's hand and wrote something on her palm. "I've got to run. I'm meetin' my boyfriend in a few minutes." She waggled her eyebrows. "I snagged myself a veterinarian."

"Congratulations." Sam used her napkin to wipe her skin where Alison had written. "See you."

Eli waited until Alison had left. "Who was that?"

Sam rolled her eyes. "We went to high school together. Alison was a mean girl then. Probably still is. I was one of her favorite targets."

Why did his mark have to be someone who'd had it rough her whole life? The half cheeseburger he'd already eaten churned in his stomach.

The waitress set their check in the middle of the table. Sam snatched it up before Eli could. "I'll be right back." She slid out of the booth and strode toward the cashier.

Making sure Sam had her back to him, Eli opened her sketchpad and quickly paged through it. Until he came to a rough drawing of a brooch in an open jewelry box. She'd colored the center stone blue. Had to be the piece her father left to her.

Eli snapped a photo of the drawing with his phone then quickly shut the sketchpad.

"What are you doing?"

He froze at Sam's question. How much had she seen? He wiped the table with his napkin. "There was some condensation on the table. I think I got it up before it reached your sketchbook."

She eyed him and then glanced down at the table as if trying to decide whether to believe him. After several beats, she squared her shoulders. "I should get back to the store." Without sitting down, she packed up her things.

"I can go with you," he offered. "I have time."

"Nope." Sam slung her bag over her shoulder. "Thanks for your help earlier. I've got it from here."

Damn it. He'd screwed it all up.

# Chapter Three

Sam's jaw tightened as she exited the diner and strode down Whiskers Lane back to Eye of Newt. Why had she accepted Eli's help at the store? Yet again, she'd thrown caution to the wind and had begun trusting a man, just that quick. Would she never learn?

He'd walked into the store the very moment Sam had realized she was in over her head. It was a little weird that he'd just offered to help her. What kind of person had time to do that? Everyone had somewhere to go, something to do. But not Eli.

Her instincts about people had always been flawed, and the fact that she'd caught Eli peeking at her drawings after she'd specifically told him no…well, that confirmed that he couldn't be trusted.

More than one of her ex-boyfriends had lied to her, said they were going to stick around and then disappeared at the first little bump in the road. How many times had her mother insisted she was clean, only to OD a week, a day, or even a few hours later? Time after time, her father had promised he was coming to visit then neglected to show.

Heck, even Aunt Emma hadn't always been honest with her, although her aunt's falsehoods weren't nearly as bad as those her parents told her. Emma's brand of dishonesty had been the protective variety—like telling Sam that her mother hadn't stolen the money from Sam's piggy bank, or that her father hadn't shown up for Sam's birthday because his flight had been canceled on account of bad weather.

Didn't much matter *why* people had deceived her. Point was, too many betrayals and lies should have soured her on the whole benefit-of-the-doubt thing. Trusting that a stranger like Eli was on the up and up was just plain stupid.

"Sam!" Eli shouted from behind her.

She couldn't just ignore him. The guy had been kind to her, up until the moment he'd peeked at her sketchpad.

When he'd touched her hand at Purry's, she couldn't deny that she'd felt something. Or that she'd noticed every woman in the diner checking him out. She couldn't blame them. Not that his looks should matter. Just because he was hot didn't mean he wasn't dangerous. What law said that ax murderers couldn't be incredibly handsome, and charming? And smell really great.

"Sam," he said again, this time from a lot closer.

What could he want from her? She barely had a dollar to her name. Perhaps she'd overreacted. How bad could he be? She shouldn't have bolted from the diner without any explanation. Now he probably thought she was twelve shades of crazy.

She stopped, drew a deep breath then turned

to face him. “Sorry I left you there, but—”

“You don’t owe me an apology. It’s me who should be sorry.” He took off his sunglasses and leveled those amazing eyes at her—not the eyes of an ax murderer. His brows angled in an upside-down vee.

“I saw you looking at my sketchpad after I’d explicitly told you no.”

“I don’t know what I was thinking.” He scrubbed a hand over his face. “The pictures you showed me were so amazing. I guess my curiosity got the best of me. I wanted to see more.”

Hardly the crime of the century. Yeah, she’d definitely overreacted. “I’m super private about my artwork.”

He held up his hands in surrender. “And you have every right to that.”

Tucking her hair behind her ear, she sighed. “When I was a kid, I had to hide my drawings from my mom. She said I was wasting my time. I had no talent, and even if I did, I’d never be able to make a living out of art.” Her old wounds were still thick with scar tissue.

Eli frowned. “You’ve got so much talent, though.”

She shrugged. “I’d be better if I’d been able to go to college to study art.”

“No reason you couldn’t do that now.”

She rolled her eyes at his naivety. “I barely made it through high school. Always being on the move—town to town, school to school, or relying on a part-time tutor who traveled with the carnival—it was impossible to learn much. Heck, a lot of the time I was supposed to be doing schoolwork, I was taking care of my mother, nursing her through a hangover or dealing with her depression. By the time Mom dumped me with Aunt Emma, I was so far behind at school."

Muscles around his jaw ticked. "I'm sorry, Sam."

She didn't want his pity. "It is what it is. I'll figure something out at the store." She doubted that, but she couldn't rely on the kindness of a stranger any longer.

"I don't mind helping you out. Hanging around an attractive lady isn't difficult. In fact, it's one of my favorite pastimes." He gave her that disarming grin. "Seriously, it's no problem. I like you."

She was definitely beginning to like him, too. Which would only make it that much harder when he inevitably left. Because everyone eventually did.

He backed away. "You know what? I'm pushing myself on you. I don't want to do that. You don't know me from Adam."

The town's Cat Officer passed them going the other way, pushing a stroller that held an orange tabby. "Afternoon."

God, Sam had missed Cat's Paw Cove.

"You like it here, don't you?" Eli asked. He seemed more tuned in to her than anyone she'd met in ages.

"I do." She'd always felt comfortable there, the one place where somebody loved her. Stopping at the entrance to Calico Court, Sam faced Eli and offered her hand. "Thanks again for all your help today."

Wearing a puzzled expression, he stared down at her hand before shaking with her. "Sure you don't want me to stay?"

"I'll manage." She couldn't take up any more of his time.

He took a gum wrapper out of his pocket and wrote something on it. "Here's my number. Would you give me a call later?"

Did he mean if she needed help, or that he wanted her to call him for other, more personal reasons? No, she had zero interest in that. Taking the paper, she slipped it into her bag. "Um, we'll see."

Eli frowned. "I wish you luck, Samantha."

She'd need it. "I'll be fine."

As soon as Sam made it to the door of the shop, a gray-haired woman sitting on the bench in front of the store stood up and tapped her watch. "I've been here for twenty minutes. Where's the lady who runs this place? I bet she didn't give you permission to leave in the middle of the day, did she? You just can't count on hired help these days."

Sam unlocked the door, ignoring the woman's insult. "The owner is my aunt. She had to go out of town."

The woman stood up with the help of a cane, brushed past Sam, and went inside. "I'll be telling Emma about your long, late lunch when she returns."

Whatever. "Yes, ma'am." Sam went inside and stashed her bag under the counter.

The elderly woman crooked her neck to look into the back room. "I take it that you don't do psychic readings like Emma does."

"No, ma'am, although they have psychic readers next door at Claws-N-Coifs, or a few blocks away at the Cheshire Apothecary."

The woman waved off Sam's suggestions.

"Emma told me that everyone in her family had that sort of gift." She narrowed her eyes at Sam. "What do you have to say to that?"

Sam flashed back to a long-ago family Thanksgiving. She couldn't have been more than seven or eight years old.

*Grandma was setting the table without lifting a finger since she had the power to move objects with her mind.*

*Uncle Henry swallowed the last of his whiskey—his third one. He crooked his finger at Sam, urging her to join him on the sofa.*

*Sam hurried to him, her mouth already watering at the prospect of one of those wrapped butterscotch candies he often gave her.*

*Henry patted the cushion for her to sit. "You sure you don't have any magic, child? All the women and girls have got something. Emma can see into the future, and Aunt Flora can heal people with her touch. Your great granny had the power to see and hear things that were way far away, a little like your mom's gift of hearing things from the spiritual realm."*

But Sam had no special gifts, nothing magic like the rest of her relatives.

"Well?" The elderly woman hit her fist on the counter. "Are you deaf?" the woman asked.

It was the same question Sam's mother had always asked her when Sam didn't immediately jump up to help her, although her mom had sometimes added stupidity to her queries.

*"Are you deaf or just stupid?"*

Sam shook off the memory. "I'm sorry, I can't help you. I can have Aunt Emma call you when she gets back." She set a slip of paper and a pen on the counter and pushed it toward the woman.

The woman swore under her breath as she

wrote down her information then left.

Unfortunately, Sam's memories refused to stop poking at her mind.

*"Why are you so dumb? How am I supposed to drag the midway if I can't leave you alone for a second without you screwing everything up? What a damn retard. You cost me a four-dollar piece of plush with your stupid paint. Who wants a white teddy bear with red fingerprints all over it?"*

*"I'm sorry, Mom." Sam had wanted to run back to the trailer they shared with her mother's then-boyfriend, far from the crowded midway and all the eyes boring into her, all the other carnies and the locals laughing at her. Only her mother had her by the collar. And apparently, the spectacle was bringing people over to her mom's hoop-la booth.*

The door chime jarred Sam back to the moment as another customer came in. She pasted on a smile. "Can I help you?"

The next two hours were pure torture as Sam struggled to run the register and find items customers requested. Even though most of the shoppers were nicer than the old woman, and infinitely more patient, Sam felt like a total failure. Why hadn't she swallowed her pride and asked Eli to stay and help her a little longer?

It was almost six pm when the store finally cleared out. Every muscle in Sam's body complained. She'd be a complete wreck by the time Aunt Emma returned. How in the world would she manage running the shop for the next nine days?

She had to get some help. She'd lost touch with the few friends she'd made in high school, and the only other locals she knew were the people who worked at the nearby businesses who wouldn't have time to help Sam handle the store.

She could ask Eli if he'd consider coming back in the morning, but why would he? The man had a life. Leaning on her aunt's stool behind the counter, Sam straightened the register. After the way she'd overreacted to Eli peeking at her sketchpad, he probably wanted nothing more to do with her.

Maybe there was something she could do for him, a way to repay him for his kindness—and at the same time convince him to stay on for a day, an hour, or whatever he'd agree to. Even if he couldn't help her out anymore, she owed him for the time he'd already put in.

Her eyes landed on the framed drawing of Aunt Emma hanging over the door. Sam's work was much better now than it had been when she'd made the charcoal portrait, but Emma had always loved it.

*"You give people a piece of yourself when you draw them,"* Emma had said.

Sam did have something she could give Eli—her art. Without a moment's hesitation, she hurried out to her car and retrieved her paint-splattered tackle box from the trunk. Minutes later, she sat in the back room of the store and started sketching Eli from memory on a piece of craft paper.

She used hard and soft pastels, for his eyes—celadon and seafoam; mocha, cypress, and cinnamon for his hair and the shadow of stubble on his face. Studying her work-in-progress, she knew she was missing something—but what? She added sparkle to his eyes, dimples on either side of his mouth. Details always came back to her when she drew from memory, stuff she hadn't realized that she'd noticed.

Would she ever see him again? Regret tugged at her insides. Getting his help at the herb shop was only part of the reason. She'd liked him—a lot. He'd been so kind to her, for no reason in particular. That made him a rarity in her world.

The guys she'd met in the last few years always wanted something from her—usually sex. After they got it, they stopped even the most basic polite gestures.

Eli had seemed different as if he genuinely cared. Why had she insisted she could do this without him? Because she liked him too much. And whenever she started counting on anyone, they left her. They always did. So why bother getting too comfortable having him around? But she needed his help.

As she sketched and added in colors and shading, her fragile confidence returned. Doing what she loved—what she was good at—filled her with happiness. Almost an hour had passed when she checked the time again. A few more touches and she quit for the time being.

After locking the door, she phoned Eli. When his voicemail picked up, she nearly disconnected, but she wanted him to have the sketch after she finished it later. "Eli, hi. I made you something. Give me a call, and I'll drop it off to you, or you can come by and pick it up. Oh, this is Samantha, by the way." She hung up, shaking her head at her awkward message. Maybe he'd call back, maybe he wouldn't. She packed up her art supplies, counted out the register, and put the money in Emma's bank bag. Would her aunt pay her for working at the store? The thought brought with it a stab of guilt, considering everything Emma had done for her.

Glimpsing the empty wall space above the herb jars gave her an idea. Aunt Emma wouldn't mind if Sam hung some of her work there. Lots of restaurants and gift shops were decorated with art that was for sale. Why not at Eye of Newt? Her aunt would forgive her a few nails in the wall that could easily be patched.

She headed to her car to grab some of her work. A few minutes later, she had the first three pieces hung—two still lifes and her newest painting, a portrait of her father that she'd done from an old photograph. She'd added in the sapphire brooch he'd left her since that was all she had of him, although she hadn't gotten the jewel's faceting just right. If she sold that picture, she'd paint another rendition to keep. She moved the stepladder over and was about to climb up and hammer in more nails when her cell rang. Absently, she answered. "Hello?"

"You have something for me, hmm?" Eli asked. "What is it?"

A shiver of excitement danced over her skin. "You'll have to wait and see." She held the phone closer to her ear and offered up a wish that he'd suggest coming by the store in the morning, or better still, tonight.

"Now, you've piqued my curiosity."

She imagined the rich timbre of his voice as colors—moss green, sienna, and midnight blue. Since when did just talking to a guy on the phone make her stomach do flips? She did want his help at the store, but more than that, she had a desire to see him again. The sooner, the better. "I'll make you a deal."

He laughed. "A deal? How could I refuse?"

Pleasant heat coursed through her. "You shouldn't. I think I sort of ruined your lunch. How about you let me make it up to you over dinner?" At his silence, she crossed her fingers. "Unless you've already eaten."

"No, I haven't. I'd like that."

The cat café would be closing in half an hour, and most of the other restaurants in town were out of her price range. She could invite him to her aunt's house. Emma's note had said that she'd left plenty of food for Sam in the fridge.

Normally she wouldn't ask someone she'd just met, but if Eli had wanted to, he could have stolen cash from the shop's register when she'd gone to the bathroom, or even when she was busy helping customers. He hadn't.

"I could fix us dinner. I'm a good cook."

"Sounds like a plan. Can I bring anything?"

"Nope. Just yourself. Give me an hour to clean up."

After texting him the address and locking up the store, she drove the short distance to her aunt's house in The Cove subdivision. Sam used the flashlight app on her phone to find the spare key under the same flowerpot where Emma had always kept it. She let herself in, taking a moment to breathe in the familiar scent of the dried lavender her aunt had in crystal bowls throughout the cottage. Nothing had changed in the years since Sam had last been there, from the colorful crocheted afghan over the rocking chair in the living room, to the umbrella stand in the front hall that held a few umbrellas and one old handmade broom.

She shut her eyes and let the memories wrap around her like a warm, wooly coat: losing at Scrabble to her aunt at the small kitchen table, having a sleepover with a friend from school, the first time

Sam had ever done that. She recalled sitting on the sofa watching a movie with the boy she'd liked, under her aunt's watchful eye; unwrapping her gift on her fourteenth birthday, her first set of good paints, the best thing her aunt—or anyone else—had ever given her.

Ginger—Aunt Emma's orange tabby strode toward Sam and stretched as if she'd recently awakened from a long nap.

"Just as pretty as ever, sweet girl." Sam crouched to pet the feline, who purred in response. As Sam headed into the kitchen, the cat weaved a path ahead, trying to steer Sam to the set of silver bowls on the floor in the corner.

"I know," Sam said. "You're hungry. We're going to take care of that right now." After she'd fixed a soupy mixture of wet cat food and water for Ginger—per Aunt Emma's instructions—Sam headed down the hall.

Her old bedroom was exactly as she'd left it, only neater. Same colorful flowered bedspread and matching curtains. Smiling, she set her bags on the bed. She had just enough time for a quick shower before Eli arrived.

Fifteen minutes later, dressed in jeans and a T-shirt, she dug in her suitcase and fished out the black velvet pouch that held the brooch. She loosened the drawstring and removed the small plastic box. Every time she looked at the midnight-blue stone, she was struck by how the jewel glittered as if it had somehow pulled all the light within a mile into itself.

Last time she'd visited her dad—a couple of years ago—he'd said that the brooch was hundreds of years old, and had belonged to a Scottish noblewoman. No telling if that was true, or the part about the sapphire having magical powers. It wasn't that she doubted the notion of magic. Heck, she'd witnessed all sorts of otherworldly powers right in her own family. But she'd yet to test the powers of the piece.

She wished she could contact her aunt and find out why Emma hadn't wanted Sam to make any decisions about the sapphire until they spoke. Weeks ago, Aunt Emma had wired her four hundred bucks to get her through until she'd been paid for the mural in Virginia. That money was nearly gone now.

What if her dad had been telling the truth about the sapphire? Was it possible that it could stop someone from lying? She held the brooch against her chest and racked her brain to think up a lie. She had to giggle at the first thing that came to mind. "I don't find Eli…" Her throat seized up as she tried to utter the last word—attractive.

A chill rolled over her skin. "I don't find Eli…" She couldn't finish the sentence. It was as if she had laryngitis.

*Because it's a lie.*

The sapphire really was magic. Her heart raced. Before she could test the stone's magic with a different lie, headlights hopscotched through the window. Teasing back the curtain, she saw Eli's car next to hers. She returned the jewel to its pouch and stashed it in a vase on the dresser. Then she went to answer the door barefoot, hair still tangled and damp.

Eli was also wearing jeans. A green polo shirt emphasized his broad shoulders. He gave her that disarming smile, dimples and all.

She ignored the pleasant ache low in her belly, and she stepped aside. "Come on in."

He handed her two bottles as he brushed past her. "I didn't know what you were cooking, so I hedged my bets."

Ginger appeared out of nowhere to inspect the stranger.

Eli chuckled and petted the cat's back. "Who's this?"

"That's Ginger," Sam supplied. "She thinks she owns the place, which of course, she does. And don't put your keys down where she can get them. She has a bad habit of stealing things."

"Nice to meet you, Ginger, you little thief."

The feline meowed up at him and rubbed against his shins. Then she ran off as if on an important mission.

Inhaling Eli's masculine scent, Sam's pulse kicked up a notch. "I just got out of the shower. I need a minute to get myself together."

His eyes grew dark as sin as he skimmed his gaze over her from head to toe. "I can't imagine that you could improve upon this look."

The heat of awareness seeped through her. Shutting the door, she was reminded of how heavily wooded this part of the subdivision was, which made Aunt Emma's cottage invisible to the neighbors. Had it been a mistake to invite Eli here?

Getting involved with a man she'd just met—someone who was completely not her type—was the most reckless thing she could do. For heaven's sake. She hadn't even been back in town for twenty-four hours.

She suddenly remembered the reading Mallory

had given her earlier. She'd said something about a whirlwind romance, and she'd warned Sam that the guy couldn't be trusted. She drew a steadying breath. Had she made a mistake by inviting Eli to her aunt's secluded cabin?

# Chapter Four

Eli mentally kicked himself. Instead of putting Sam at ease, he'd allowed his attraction for her to show. Now he'd first have to calm the wariness he saw in her eyes before he could even attempt to get her to trust him. He had to remember that she was his mark, not a potential lover. When she turned her back on him and set the wine on the counter, he took a backward step, putting a little more space between them. "Sure you don't want to go out to eat? I hate for you to go to any trouble. And to be perfectly honest, I can tell you're nervous about being alone with me. I can assure you that I won't turn into a werewolf. That only happens to me where there's a full moon."

She faced him, eyeing him for several moments, and the crease of her brow gradually smoothed out. Her tense stance relaxed, although she hadn't even cracked a smile at his joke. "This is fine, as long as it's okay with you."

"A home-cooked meal? Yeah, it's great." He rubbed his hands together and followed Sam a few steps to a postage-stamp-size kitchen. "What can I do to help with dinner?"

"What are werewolves good at?" Finally, she smiled.

"Good question. Tearing stuff apart? Trying to fool little girls in red cloaks?"

Sam rolled her eyes. "That was a regular old wolf, not a werewolf."

"I failed fairytales in kindergarten."

She took down two glasses from the overhead rack. "Opener is in the drawer next to the stove. Either bottle's fine. I'll be back in a sec. Then I'll check out Aunt Emma's fridge for ingredients."

"An improvising chef. Impressive."

A grin lifted one corner of her mouth. "You should probably wait to see what I come up with before you start handing me compliments." With that, she strode from the room.

Eli uncorked the Chardonnay while he scanned the kitchen. Had Sam taken the time to hide the brooch? The kitchen would be a logical place. With a bunch of shelves packed with various containers, a refrigerator full of food, and drawers and cabinets that were probably crammed with all sorts of the junk people stashed away, it would take him hours to search the room. No, he wouldn't be able to merely rummage through the cottage and find the sapphire. He'd have to gain her trust to get her to tell him where she was keeping it.

Sam returned with her hair a little drier, the curls already starting to poof. She still smelled just as wonderful as she had before—like patchouli and sweet orange, scents he was now familiar with after several hours of mixing essential oils for her aunt's customers.

Picking up one of the wine glasses he'd filled, she took a sip. "Mm. That's good." She closed her eyes for a moment and drew a deep breath then exhaled slowly. "Wine and a hot shower. It doesn't get much better than that."

"I know today was difficult for you. I'm sorry if I added any tension."

She widened her eyes. "You? Seriously? I'd have never gotten through it without your help. It was challenging, though. A few of the customers took me for an incompetent idiot because I wasn't able to find what they were looking for in a nanosecond. One of them actually said so to my face." Her brow furrowed for a moment. She took another drink. "Doesn't matter. Growing up with a mother who constantly hurled insults at me, I grew a thick skin."

A weight constricted his chest. "That doesn't make it right."

Shrugging, she set her glass down and opened the fridge. "Gotta love Aunt Emma. Looks like she's still doing her shopping at a wholesale club and buying enough to feed an army."

With Sam engrossed in figuring out their menu, this would be a great opportunity to snoop around. "Mind if I use your restroom?" he asked.

Without taking her head out of the refrigerator, she said, "Second door on the left."

He wasted no time checking out the bathroom medicine cabinet. Nothing but the usual suspects there. With a glance toward the kitchen, he quietly padded to the room across the hall. The light and ceiling fan was on. The open suitcase on the bed and a tackle box dotted with paint on the floor told him it was Sam's room. An uncomfortable heaviness pressed his abdomen.

He held perfectly still and listened. From the kitchen, pots clanged, and an electric mixer or blender turn on. With Sam occupied, he seized the moment to quickly search her suitcase but came up empty—except for his remorse over invading her privacy.

When the appliance noise stopped, he slipped out of the bedroom and made his way back to the kitchen. A painting on the wall in the hallway caught his eye—a little girl with auburn curls sat on a blanket on the beach, dwarfed by dunes and seagrass. There was something so sad and lonely about the child. Even the muted browns and moss greens scrub palms evoked such a gloomy feel. The initials in the bottom right corner were painted in white—SC. His eyes burned as he focused on the girl.

"Did you fall in?"

He jumped at Sam's voice. Standing in the kitchen doorway holding her wine, she tucked her hair behind her ear, giving him a better view of her long, graceful neck and a silver hoop earring.

"Sorry." He tipped his chin toward the painting. "This is your work, right?"

"Mm-hmm. Not my best, but one Aunt Emma fell in love with."

"I have to agree with your aunt. It's very good. Incredibly lonely, though."

Her eyes hooded. "Guess I captured the mood of my childhood, at least the time when I was with my mother."

He swallowed past the lump in his throat. Damn it. He couldn't let emotions get in the way of the job he had to do. The consequences of failure would be more than he could bear. He forced his thoughts to Lizzy, and what could happen to her if he didn't do what Rodrigo wanted. He conjured an image of his sister, helpless in her wheelchair, unable to defend herself from those vicious thugs. Fear twisted in his gut, until he tamped down all thoughts of Lizzy, and met Sam's stare. "Sounds like you've been cooking up a storm in there."

She shrugged. "Easy stuff. I hope you like eggs. And tomatoes. We're having a frittata and garlic-cheese bread."

"Sounds delicious." While she checked on their dinner, he refilled her wine. Alcohol might loosen her up enough to confide in him. Handing her the glass, he savored the aromas of basil, oregano, and cheese. "Smells great. What can I do to help?"

"Set the table." She handed him napkins and forks, their fingers touching for a brief moment. Their gazes met and held, and sparks charged the atmosphere between them. Until Sam broke the connection and turned away.

Liking her wasn't part of the plan. Feelings would only complicate his mission.

She plated the frittata and set out a basket of bread. Gesturing toward one of the simple wooden chairs, she sat opposite Eli. "Dig in."

The food was as good as any he'd had at five-star hotels in Nevada or Atlantic City. After they finished eating, he insisted on doing the dishes. That done, he opened the pinot noir and brought their glasses to the living room sofa.

Sam hesitated. "I'm pretty tired."

If she fell asleep while he was there, he could slip back to her room and hopefully find the jewel. Then he could get the hell out of there and not have to face her. Better that he should quickly rip off the bandage rather than prolong their time together. "Just one nightcap?"

A slow smile settled on her lips. "You drive a hard bargain." She took the wine from him and drank. Her eyes were getting glassy. "I don't indulge very often, and hardly ever this much, thanks to my mother's addictive habits. This stuff is way better than I've had in a long time, though. Maybe ever."

He'd been nursing his drink all night, which he doubted she'd noticed, although if he got buzzed, maybe his mission—and the fact that Sam was going to be destroyed by it—wouldn't be so difficult to swallow. He settled in next to her and tapped his glass to hers. "So, tell me more about Samantha. You said your mom and your aunt took turns raising you. Was your father in the picture at all?"

The furrow of her brow reflected unhealed emotional scars. "Not much. Dad was a lot older than my mother. They were only married for about five minutes. Mom kicked him out while I was still in diapers. He called me three years ago, said he wanted to rebuild our relationship."

At least someone else besides her aunt had cared about her.

"But then he died a couple years later." She took a healthy swallow of wine. Ginger jumped onto the sofa and curled up on Sam's lap as if the cat sensed Sam's emotions.

He patted the cat's head. "I'm sorry. Was he an artist like you?"

"He was a gemologist, traveled around the country going to gem and mineral shows." Her eyes widened. *"That's* what I got from him. I've been wandering my whole life. I've always been a bit of a rolling stone." She smiled at her joke.

"Cute." He couldn't tear his gaze from her pretty face. Those cornflower eyes sparkled. When she smiled, it was like the sun peeking through the clouds after a spring rain. A heavy silence hung in the space between them. Until he reminded himself that he was there for a reason. "A gemologist. Sounds interesting."

She rolled her eyes. "Never was to me. But maybe that's because he seemed to care more about his amethyst cathedrals and his Dominican amber specimens than he did about me."

Forcing himself to ignore the tug at his chest, he continued drawing her out. "I'm sure you were more important to him than gems. Did he ever give you any that you liked?"

She caught her bottom lip between her teeth and stared at him for several seconds. Did she suspect anything?

"He left me one in his will," she finally answered. "A magic sapphire brooch. When someone holds it or wears it, they can't tell a lie." A sad smile settled on her lips. "From the man who repeatedly lied to me. I might not be able to spell irony, but I know it when I hear it."

The confirmation that she had the jewel was more bitter than sweet. "Sounds intriguing, if you believe in that sort of stuff. Have you ever tested it?" Would this be so easy as merely asking her to show him the gemstone?

Her lips bunched to one side, but she didn't say anything. After several beats, she brightened. "I almost forgot. I have something for you." She set the cat aside and sprung off the sofa, disappearing from the room.

Eli scanned the living room in search of anything that might be a hiding spot for the sapphire. Unfortunately for him, Sam's aunt was apparently one of those people with numerous collections. A dozen or more small pendulums hung from the curtain rods over both windows; several shelves held boxes of tarot cards and crystal balls on pedestals; baskets of all shapes and sizes were scattered all over the room. He'd never find something so small as a brooch in a hoarder's paradise like her aunt's house.

If he couldn't get Sam to reveal where the sapphire was, he'd be forced to break in when she wasn't there, and search everything. Another potential crime to add to his resume.

While she was gone, he filled her glass almost to the rim. That invisible weight he hadn't been able to shake, kept pressing on him.

Sam came back carrying a black zippered portfolio and set it on the coffee table in front of him. Her chest rose and fell with a deep breath before she sat down and opened the zipper. "I really hope you like this." She pulled out a large sketchpad, opened it to the middle, and handed it to Eli. "It's not a hundred percent finished yet, but I wanted you to see it."

She'd made a drawing of him. The vise around his insides squeezed tighter. "This is incredible, Sam." She'd captured him perfectly, almost like a photo, but with more depth and emotion. Her technique reminded him of the drawings and paintings at a museum exhibit Lizzy had taken him to when he was a kid. Contemporary realism, his sister had called the style.

Only his face was done in Sam's drawing, but the way she'd drawn his eyes was startling. They appeared to look straight at him—or rather, through him, accusing him. His own guilt stared back at him. He swallowed hard and straightened. "I can't believe you did this, and so fast. I love it."

She waved off his praise. "Not everyone is okay with being drawn." She took a sip of her wine. "Sometimes, I can't help myself." She flipped a few sheets forward to a pencil drawing of a middle-aged woman sitting on a park bench. "Like this lady I sketched when I was living in upstate New York. I was hoping she might buy it. But oh my God, she freaked out when she saw it. She started saying stuff about suing me and invading her privacy."

And he knew why. Sam had a knack for capturing the essence of her subjects, which was a little disconcerting, especially for people with something to hide.

Closing the tablet, she sighed. "I grabbed my supplies and ran. I mean, I don't have a pot, if you know what I mean. I sure as heck don't need a lawsuit."

But she did have *something* valuable. And he was going to steal from her. He took a sip of wine to wash away the bitter taste in the back of his throat.

"Makes you wonder what's beneath the surface, you know?"

He shook his head. "I'm not sure I understand what you mean."

She closed her eyes for a second. "Like she probably had a reason for being so suspicious of me. Maybe someone had invaded her privacy before, and that was why she was so uptight about me drawing her." A wry grin brightened her expression. "Or she was on the lam for…murdering her lover or stealing millions from the company she worked for. Everyone has a story, stuff they're hiding."

He forced a chuckle, yet her observation had struck a nerve with him. "You have quite an imagination."

Her eyelids were droopy. She was getting tipsy. "I don't know about that. You never can tell what people are really about. Most wear masks some of the time, others always do."

His mouth was suddenly dry as dust. "You think everyone's dishonest?"

She drained her glass. "Everyone I've dealt with."

"What about your Aunt Emma? You said she took you in, helped raise you."

"She did, and she also candy-coated a lot of things. Her lies were white, but they were still dishonest." Her eyes went liquid. "My mother always denied she'd been doing drugs, and time after time, my father promised he was coming to see me for a birthday or Christmas. He never did. Only lies. All the guys I've dated either cheated or lied or left me when they promised to hang around. I guess that's just what people do."

He wanted to deny it, tell her that there were good people in the world, but he'd rarely encountered any. And he was destined to earn a spot on her list of people who'd deceived her. God, he hated himself for it.

"Want some more wine?" Sam stood up, wobbling as she did. "Whew."

Eli reached for her arm to steady her, but before he could get her, she practically collapsed, half on the cushion, half on him.

She stayed there for a moment until a rosy flush crawled up her neck and face. She shifted off of him. "Whoops. Sorry about that."

He wasn't. What was the matter with him? She was the very last woman in the world he should be attracted to. Another reason to disappear from her life as soon as he got the brooch.

Instead of standing, she leaned against his shoulder. "You smell good."

Summoning all his restraint, he started to move away. Until Sam hooked her hand around his neck and pulled him closer. Their eyes were an inch apart.

His heartbeat pounded in his ears. He blocked everything out of his mind. There was no mission, no loan shark, no threats. Only the fascinating woman he was starting to like way more than he had a right to.

Then her lips were on his. He circled his arms around her waist and drew her against him. She tasted of good wine and innocence. And he wanted more. He cupped her face, caressing her satiny skin, running his thumb over the pale freckles on her cheek, deepening the kiss.

Sam broke contact and her lips—still swollen and red from their kiss—moved as if she was trying to formulate words.

He didn't want to hear the reasons why they shouldn't; they'd just met, hardly knew each other. Hell, he had way more cause to stop than Sam did, but he yearned for more. He pressed his lips to hers for another taste and drank in her sweetness.

Her pleasured moan assured him they were on the same page. She climbed onto his lap, facing him. If they didn't stop, he wouldn't be able to stand up. And he couldn't let this go too far. He kissed the tip of her nose, her forehead, then eased her off of him.

Her puzzled expression cut through him. As much as he desired her, making love to her now would make him the worst kind of jerk. "We shouldn't."

The pulse at her temples fluttered. "I thought…"

Gathering her hands in his, he kissed her fingers. "You thought right, believe me. But…I've got an early meeting tomorrow."

The excuse didn't do much to ease the disappointment in her expression. He'd wounded her already-fragile ego. Another transgression against her. The list was growing.

Unless… Maybe he could convince Rodrigo to give him a different assignment, some other task to pay back his debt. There had to be something else Diaz wanted. Or he could try to up the limit on his credit card and take a cash advance to pay part of his gambling debt. His Visa was maxed out from paying the private duty nurse after Lizzy had fallen several months ago. It was already going to take him years to get out of debt, so what did it matter if he added more? He'd do anything to get out of hurting Sam.

He kissed her cheek.

Her lips flattened to a thin line. "That feels like goodbye."

The disillusionment in her eyes ripped through him. "No, Sam, not at all. How about I come by the shop tomorrow? I can help you with the customers. As soon as I'm finished with my meeting."

She brightened. "That'd be great."

"I love the drawing."

Glancing toward her sketchpad, she shrugged one shoulder. "It'll be better when I'm done with it."

"I can't wait to see it." Rather than torture himself anymore, he got up. "I should be going."

"Yeah, I guess you should. See you tomorrow?"

"Definitely." He headed out, and as soon as he started his car, he checked the time. Didn't matter that it was past eleven. Rodrigo's evening exploits were probably just beginning, although Eli couldn't care less if he woke him up. He called the contact number that he'd been given on the flash drive.

Diaz's voicemail picked up after several rings.

A light went on in one of Sam's windows. Her pretty blue eyes flashed in his mind, her soft lips and the earthy scent of her skin. He cleared his throat and backed out of the parking spot. "Mr. Diaz, this is Eli Kincaid. I'd like a different…assignment. This one isn't going to work out. I'm sure we can come to an agreement about what I can do for you. Call me." He hung up as he pulled onto the main road just outside the subdivision. For good measure, he fished out his lucky poker chip and closed it in his fist. "Please let this work," he murmured.

Minutes later he checked into the Palmetto Motel, a dive a few miles outside of town. The dingy room was all he'd expected a thirty-dollar-a-night place would be—yellowed paint, 1960-style lamps and a bed that appeared to have seen more action than Ron Jeremy and John Holmes combined. Didn't matter. He had more important things on his mind.

After a long shower with lousy water pressure, he pulled off the threadbare bedspread and sat on the bed. His cell signaled a message. He called his voicemail and listened. "That's a good one, Kincaid," Rodrigo said in the message. "You're a funny guy. Unfortunately for you, this isn't the labor pool. You don't get to choose another job. So you'd better find what we discussed, or my associates will be paying a visit to your sister. Sven likes Atlanta. And Manny's real *handy* with a paper cutter, if you catch my drift."

"Shit!" Eli threw the phone across the bed, then paced the stained carpet. There had to be a solution. Nothing came to him, so after several minutes, he turned on his laptop and logged into his bank account. He found a phone number to call for inquiring about raising his credit limit. He'd try that in the morning. If he could give Rodrigo half or even a third of what he owed him, he prayed the old shark would cut him a break and give him more time to pay the rest. If he could secure a cash advance, maybe he could work on Sam, and talk her into selling the brooch to him. Then he'd give Rodrigo what he wanted, and Lizzy would remain safe.

One thing he knew for sure—he already cared about Sam, and he couldn't betray her.

# Chapter Five

Sam unlocked the door to Eye of Newt a few minutes before ten two days later. Instead of focusing on the endless number of white labels with difficult words on every bottle and drawer, she admired her paintings on the walls above them. Although her artwork alone wasn't responsible for her good mood. Eli had spent hours yesterday and the day before helping her at the store. Every time the shop had emptied of customers, they'd flirted with each other and had even shared a kiss or two in the back room. Sometime today he'd come by again, or so he'd promised yesterday. Anticipation tingled up her spine.

Granted she had a bad habit of jumping into relationships with guys, which had bitten her in the ass a few times. Yet Eli seemed different—completely opposite her usual blue-collar, tatted up kind of dude. If she was honest, though, her usual type hadn't worked out so well for her. She'd had two relationships in the past year—each lasting only a few months. And both had left her lonelier than the previous one.

Not that she was looking for a boyfriend. Heck no. She only planned to stay in town long enough to replenish her bank account and to spend time with Aunt Emma after she returned home.

Stashing her bag under the counter, she sighed. That first day she'd been not only terrified about working at the shop by herself but also a little lonely. Eli was just what the doctor ordered for both problems. So what that she hardly knew him? Her instincts told her that Eli was completely different, more caring, and thoughtful than the other guys. Then again, her intuition had been a little off before—or more like broken beyond repair. Too bad that she didn't have her great aunt Sunny's intuition about people, or even Aunt Emma's gift of divining the future.

Eli seemed so willing to help her like there was nothing he'd rather be doing. Which she was beyond grateful for. Although it had crossed her mind that he might not continue coming by every day. If he needed convincing, she could employ the methods she'd seen her mother use so many times when Sam was growing up. Like when the carnival manager had threatened to fire her after she'd overdosed on painkillers. Her mom had sat on the man's lap and whispered in his ear—no doubt making him promises of sexual favors.

Not that Sam would sleep with Eli to get his help, but she wasn't above a little flirtation. She'd never been much good at the subtleties of that type of behavior, and her conscience would prevent her from using him that way. In truth, she was enjoying her make-out sessions with Eli. He was an attractive guy. But she knew better than to get too used to having him around.

Since no one was beating down the door, she used the time to work on her picture of Eli. She shaded his face with beige, light peach, and pink blush. Burnt ochre created a five o'clock shadow below his nose and along his jawline. As she worked on his mouth, she couldn't help but recall his kisses, and the taste of his tongue. A flicker of heat bloomed inside her.

The door chime interrupted her thoughts. Sam wiped her hands on a rag. "Welcome," she said to the young woman.

"Who's the artist?" The brunette pointed to one of the paintings on the wall.

"I am."

The woman slowly walked past the pictures, stopping under each one and spending several moments with it. "You're good. My mom's an interior decorator up in Gainesville. Mind if I take photos of these and send them to her? She's always picking up works from up-and-coming artists for her clients."

Sam's pulse quickened at the prospect of making a sale, or more than one. "Please, go ahead. I've got others I haven't put up yet."

"Thanks. I'll text her these. Maybe she can come to see the rest if she's interested." After paying, she left.

Although she didn't buy a painting herself, the woman gave Sam hope that her work could sell there. She couldn't wait to share the news with Eli.

When the door opened again a few minutes later, he came inside, arms loaded down with a paper tray that held two coffee cups, a square bakery box, and a plastic shopping bag. "Morning." His gaze tracked over her body so fast that she'd have missed it if she hadn't been looking at him.

The heat of awareness flooded her system. She hadn't drunk any champagne in a long time, but her stomach felt as bubbly as if she'd just had a couple glasses. She closed the distance between them and took the coffees from him. "Actually it's afternoon."

"I had some errands to run. I guess time got away from me." He set the box on the counter. "I picked up some stuff from the bakery a few blocks away. Hope you like chocolate-cherry tortes. Not a very nutritious lunch, but I couldn't resist."

Glimpsing the bakery name on the top of the box, she squealed excitedly. "Ooh, Sugarland." She opened the package and inhaled the sweet scent. "They make the best. They're my favorite, any time of the day. Thank you." Maybe her instincts about him were right. At least he was thoughtful. And he smelled even better than the pastries did. Renewed desire washed over her.

Eli glanced up at one the paintings she'd added the night before. He gestured toward the picture of her father. "Tell me about that one."

"That's my dad. I started on it the night I found out he'd passed away, when I knew for sure that we'd never get a do-over for our relationship." Her eyes stung. Didn't really matter that it had been her dad's fault that they'd barely had anything to do with each other.

"Is that the brooch you were telling me about in his hand?"

She nodded. "I added that a couple weeks later after I got the jewel."

"Hmm." Lines creased his forehead as he handed her one of the coffee cups. He looked at the painting again and frowned.

Why had his mood shifted so suddenly? With her history of chasing guys away, it was likely her fault. "Everything okay?"

"Yeah, fine." But his furrowed brow made her wonder.

Before she could press him about what was on his mind, a customer came in, and then two more. Eli helped her handle the rush. Business finally slowed a couple hours later.

Eli rubbed the back of his neck. "I bet you'll sell a painting soon. A few people have made comments about how good they are."

"Seriously?" She couldn't keep herself from smiling.

"Sure. I can't believe you're not rich and famous yet. You will be, though."

Thinking about how much money she'd made recently, she had to laugh. "Living on the edge, actually. You've heard of the starving artist? That would be me."

He glanced at the paintings again. "That's hard to believe. How do you get by?"

Sam's cheeks warmed. Aunt Emma had occasionally sent her money in the last few years, but mostly she'd been living on the cheap, selling paintings and drawings, doing the occasional mural for businesses. "I manage, barely."

His lips flattened. "Feel free to tell me to shut up if this is none of my business, but why not sell that piece of jewelry you were telling me about, the one your father left you? I mean, you could put part of the money away, or buy yourself…a new car or a down payment on a house. Wouldn't your father want that for you?"

She'd considered exactly that until her aunt had warned her that selling the brooch would be a mistake. Sam had seen too many of Emma's predictions come true to doubt her, which was why she based certain decisions on her advice. And knowing that the sapphire really was magic…well, that was a game changer. "It's complicated. I just know I'm not supposed to sell it, not yet anyway."

Eli sipped his coffee. "I lost both my parents when I was a kid, and I'm sure that if they'd had anything of value to leave to my sister and me, they'd have wanted us to use that to make our life easier."

Why did he seem almost upset about her insistence that she didn't want to sell the sapphire? Maybe it had reminded him of his loss. "I didn't realize your folks had passed away. I'm sorry."

He shrugged. "It's been a long time. Doesn't bother me anymore."

"Are you close with your sister?" she asked.

"Kind of. We're half-siblings. She's a lot older than I am. She took care of me after our mother died." He rubbed the bridge of his nose, and Sam sensed the loss was still painful for him despite his statement to the contrary.

Sam squeezed his forearm. Sadness tinged his expression as he shrugged off her concern. "I understand how hard it is to lose a parent." She thought about her mother. "Even when they're still alive."

He pulled her into a hug. It felt so good to have his arms around her. She shut her eyes and leaned her head against the hard planes of his chest.

Until his cell buzzed, cutting short the intimate moment.

She wrapped her arms around herself, mourning the loss of his touch.

Eli looked at his phone and frowned. "I need to take this." He answered, then went outside.

Busying herself with dusting the apothecary cabinet, Sam glanced through the window. Eli scrubbed a hand over his face. He appeared to be arguing with the caller.

"Everything okay?" she asked when he came back inside.

"Sure, fine." His smile didn't reach his eyes. What wasn't he telling her?

A customer came into the shop, then another and another. Soon the place was as busier than it had been all week. When the rush finally ended, it was nearly four pm. Sam stretched to loosen her tense muscles. "I could use a break. Can I interest you in a Moon Pie?"

"Let's do it." Eli gestured toward the back room.

Sam grabbed two of the individually wrapped treats and joined Eli at the table.

"I guess you're as much of a health nut as I am, living on sugar and caffeine." Eli tore open the plastic and took a bite. "Mm. I haven't had one of these in at least a decade. Just as good as I remember."

She nodded. "Moon Pies never disappoint." Unlike most everything else in life.

"Did you notice how many people have been checking out your art?" he asked. "I can feel the excitement building. You're going to sell every one of them."

"That'd be nice."

"I mean that, Sam." He set down what was left of his Moon Pie and took her hand. "You've got real talent. It's like you tap into your subjects' souls. That sounds weird, but I don't know how else to explain it."

Eli wasn't the first person to say something to that effect about her work.

His phone buzzed several times, but he didn't take the calls. He just checked the display then stashed it back in his pocket.

"If you need to return a call, go ahead," she said.

He shook his head. "You're the only one I want to talk to right now."

"I bet you say that to all the girls," she teased.

With a shrug, he said, "Yeah, I do." After a few beats, he cracked a smile. "Kidding. I like being with you."

Warmth wrapped around her like a fluffy blanket. Their gazes locked and held for several seconds. Until the door chimed. Sam pushed away from the table and returned to the front of the store to help the customer. The rest of the day flew past as she and Eli worked side by side. She was starting to get the hang of where everything was, and she could probably handle most of it alone. Only she was enjoying having Eli there with her. She couldn't expect him to keep giving her all of his time, though.

"Hey," she said. "You've been a lifesaver the past couple of days. I don't know what I'd have done without you."

"It's been my pleasure, Sam." His eyes darkened as he took a step closer, and his gaze fell to her lips, turning her into a puddle of a woman.

She drew a breath laced with his scent, and suddenly it was as if a switch inside her turned on. The temperature in the room seemed to rise a dozen degrees. "I can't pay you for all you've done for me, but can I at least cook you dinner again tonight?"

He backed away and folded his arms over his chest. "Definitely not."

Had she misread his signals? Her mood clunked.

When Sam's face fell, Eli drew her into his arms. At first, she was stiff and unyielding. "Sam, I was kidding around. I don't want you to cook for me. I'd like to make *you* dinner."

Understanding softened the lines that had marred her brow. "Oh." She backed out of his embrace and shook her head. "Sometimes I'm so stupid."

"If you ask me, you're pretty smart. I was trying to be funny, but I obviously fell flat."

"I suck at reading people." She rolled her eyes.

Her self-deprecating comments cut straight through him. As if he didn't feel like the biggest heel already. Clearly, she had no confidence in herself, which was crazy considering that she was smart, talented, and gorgeous. He wanted to make her see how amazing she was.

If only the bank had agreed to raise his credit

limit, but after two days of waiting for them to reply to his request, they'd called him back a little while ago, and he'd been unable to sway neither a customer service rep nor her supervisor. He had no other way to get his hands on enough cash to buy the brooch from Sam, even if he was able to convince her to sell it to him, which was a big if.

As a last resort, he considered taking the gemstone and leaving her the money as consolation, but without the ability to get a cash advance, he was SOL. The more he contemplated that option, he realized he'd still be a jerk even if he left her payment. If it wasn't her choice to part with the jewel, he was essentially stealing it from her.

She put her hand on his shoulder. The simple touch set off sparks between them. "I'd love for you to cook me dinner," she murmured, one corner of her mouth lifting in a seductive grin.

Everything inside him yearned to take her up on her unspoken offer—everything except his conscience.

"Text me your address." She disappeared into the back room.

Now what? How could he explain his crummy lodgings? What would she think? He followed her and cleared his throat. "The place where I'm staying now…let's just say, you wouldn't want to eat anything that was prepared there."

She eyed him for a long moment. "Is that really the reason?"

The pain of past disappointments was written all over her face in invisible ink, but as someone who'd been there too—he saw it. God, he hated himself for not being completely honest with her.

"I know almost nothing about you," she said. "You don't have a wife, or a girlfriend tucked away somewhere, do you?"

"Did I neglect to mention my six wives and fifteen kids spread across four states?"

She flattened her lips to a thin line, obviously not amused.

Taking her hand, he looked deep into her eyes. "I swear that's not it."

She pulled away. "Then what is? What's your story? You've come here three days in a row. Don't you have a job or something?"

His mouth was suddenly dry as dust. He lifted his hands in surrender. "Okay, the truth. I'm staying at a fleabag motel. I'm not a nine-to-five kind of guy. I make my living playing cards, gambling if you prefer."

A ghost of a smile was there and gone in a split second. "Thanks for your honesty. What brings you to this neck of the woods? There are no casinos within at least a hundred miles."

"A card game." Technically true. His cell buzzed again. He took it out, but when he glimpsed Rodrigo's number, he immediately sent the call to voicemail, which would probably piss off the old man, but Eli didn't care to deal with the shark's insults and demands at the moment. He knew what Diaz wanted, and he was working on a solution—one that didn't involve betraying the sweet, trusting woman he was quickly growing to care for. "Would it be okay if I cooked dinner at your house, or rather, your aunt's?"

She caught her bottom lip between her teeth. Did she have any idea how sexy he found the gesture, that his brain scrambled at the mere sight? All he could think about was kissing those full, pink lips again, and so much more. Every nerve and muscle in his body strung tight.

The door to the shop chimed, and the spell was broken, at least for the time being.

"Excuse me." Sam went to help her customer.

"I'm looking for an obsidian scrying mirror," the middle-aged woman told Sam.

Sam searched the shelf where her aunt displayed similar items with no luck. "Hmm, I don't think we have that. You might try Cheshire Apothecary. That sounds like something they'd carry."

After the woman left, Sam faced Eli. "She was easy to get rid of."

He nodded. And it gave him an idea. If he told Diaz that Sam no longer had the brooch, he'd have to give Eli a different task. Could it be that simple? Diaz couldn't know if Sam had sold the jewelry to someone else, or even lost it. He had to try, for Sam's sake and his. "Are we on for dinner?"

Her expression brightened. "Sure."

The prospect that he might not be forced to betray her—and the notion of spending the evening with her, or longer—gave him hope. The weight that had been compressing his chest since he'd arrived in town, eased. He rubbed his hands together. "I should go pick up some groceries. I feel like lobster tail and champagne. What do you think?" He might be jumping the gun, but he had a good feeling about this.

She lifted an eyebrow. "Sure. What's the occasion?"

"Good things ahead for both of us." Feeling

more optimistic than he had in a week, he left the shop and strode to his car. From there he phoned Rodrigo but got his voicemail. "Mr. Diaz, it's Eli Kincaid. Sorry I missed your call. I do have some news, though. I'm afraid Samantha no longer has…the item you're looking for. She must have sold it." He considered asking if there was anything else he could do to repay the debt, but why buy trouble? Diaz would no doubt give him another illegal task, or impose some ungodly interest on the gambling debt. Anything that didn't involve Sam would be better.

With that hurdle out of the way, he turned his thoughts to planning the evening ahead—a romantic dinner with the most fascinating woman he'd met in a very long time.

# Chapter Six

Sam set the small table for two using her aunt's good china and silverware while Eli cooked. As he worked on cutting open the lobster shells, his hair slipped forward over his forehead, strand over glossy strand, and she recalled how soft that hair had felt as she'd run her fingers through it last time he'd been at the cottage. Her heart did that little fluttery thing.

He smiled at her over his shoulder. "What?"

Who wouldn't find a man like Eli attractive? Between his chiseled features and rock-solid physique, he reminded her of a male model she'd seen on billboards. "Nothing," she said. "I guess I'm impressed by all the stuff you know how to do in the kitchen."

"I'm impressive in other rooms, too." He waggled his eyebrows at her, and her legs turned to noodles.

She picked up a piece of Aunt Emma's mail from the counter and fanned herself with it.

Eli slipped the pan under the broiler. "Dinner in five minutes," he said. "I hope you like champagne."

"Sure." Tonight she was determined to limit herself to only one glass. She liked Eli a lot. Trusting him was a different story, and after growing up with an addict for a mother, she was well aware that certain substances clouded judgment. Any decisions she made tonight would be made with a clear head.

Eli handed her a champagne flute and trailed his gaze over her, and the heat of desire wound through her.

Veiling his eyes, he tapped his glass to hers. "To new friends." Clearly, he hoped they got very friendly, and Sam was't opposed to the notion.

Eli maneuvered the kitchen like a sculptor creating a masterpiece. When the oven timer dinged, he pulled out the lobster tails and set them on the stovetop. Then he topped the broccoli with homemade Hollandaise sauce, finishing it with the tiniest dash of salt. His hands moved so deftly she could hardly make out what he was doing. The way he pulled everything together at once reminded her of the guy at the carnival who worked the shell games.

The comparison jarred her like a slap of icy morning air. Eli had said he was a gambler. Did he swindle people like the carnies had? No, Eli wasn't that kind of person. In the few days she'd known him, he'd been nothing but wonderful to her. Traveling around her whole life, never staying anywhere long enough to make good friends, she'd had to size people up quickly, and every indication told her that Eli meant her no harm. So why not drown her loneliness in those strong arms? No commitment, no promise of anything more than a good time.

Eli set out a spread worthy of a fancy

restaurant—broiled lobster tails, steamed broccoli, and warm, crusty bread. While he removed the lobster meat from the shell, she lit the candles on the table.

"Dig in," he said.

Her first bite of the shellfish was heaven. She shut her eyes and moaned. "Way to sweep a girl off her feet."

There was that sexy grin of his. He raised his champagne flute. "And now I know the way to your heart." Staring at her over the rim of the glass, he drank.

A sweet ache settled low in her belly. "I think you found *many* ways. In three short days, you've repeatedly come to my rescue, cooked a gourmet dinner for me, and brought me my favorite pastry." She made a show of looking past him. "Where's your white horse?"

His eyebrows pinched tight for a moment. "I'm no knight in shining armor, Sam. You've had a lot of bad luck. You deserve better. I only want to help."

She wasn't sure how to respond. Everyone went through rough patches in their life.

They ate in silence for several minutes.

"So you like the lobster, huh?" he finally asked.

"Mm-hmm. This is only the second time I've had it. It's been at least fifteen years. I was like seven or eight last time. One of my mom's boyfriends took us to an expensive seafood restaurant in Maryland or Virginia. But they had a fight halfway through dinner, and we had to leave."

He finished his bread, eying her as he ate. "That doesn't sound like a good memory."

She set down her fork, remembering the evening so long ago. "I don't have many that are."

"I'm sorry." Eli took her hand across the table, rubbing his thumb over her knuckles. "But things improved when you came to stay with your aunt, right?"

She thought about all the back and forth time in her childhood. "Sure, it got better then."

He let go of her hand. "How'd you deal with your mom's comings and goings when you were so young?"

"Art." She smiled. "I swear, sometimes my fingers itch to hold a paintbrush or a pencil."

"Why don't you hang more of your pieces at your aunt's shop? Or rotate them. I'm sure we could fit more on the walls."

She pushed away her plate, mulling over the idea. "I only put up a few because I probably won't be here long." Now she had a reason to stay for a while—if Eli did. "I guess I could do that."

"I'll help you tomorrow." His gaze drifted lower on her body, and her inner thermostat rose. "If you want me to, that is."

"Sure, if you have time."

"I think I can squeeze you in." He threw her a playful wink. "You're a talented artist. I'd love to see you make it big. It's just…"

She straightened. "What?"

"Some of your work is…somber, lonely, you know?" He tipped his chin toward the hallway. He had to be referring to the painting her aunt had hanging next to the bathroom door. "It's still good, though. I guess I'd like you to be happier."

A lump lodged in her throat. "Once, when I

was living here with Aunt Emma, she took me to a doctor, a psychologist, who gave me pills."

He nodded. "Depression? I take them, too. It helps."

Something they had in common. "I haven't for a while." With no health insurance and no money for doctors or medicine, she'd quit taking the meds years ago, but now that she thought about it, she realized that not having the antidepressants was probably why her moods had been so up and down recently. "I should get back on them. I hate depending on anything." She lowered her gaze. "Or anyone."

Eli stood up and pulled her with him. "I joke around a lot, but I have those dark, shadowed corners in my head, too."

She cupped his cheek. "Spending time with you makes me happy. You light up those spots."

Drawing her against him, he kissed her, and she felt his need—raw and honest and sober. She wanted him, too—all of him. Splaying her hand on his chest, she broke contact and eased him back. She answered the question in his eyes, sliding her hand down his arm to thread her fingers with his. Then she led him to her room and sat on the edge of the bed. When Eli took off his shirt, she gasped at the brownish-purple bruises on his skin and tipped her chin toward his chest. "What happened? Does it hurt?"

He ran his fingers over one of the bruises. "It's nothing, really."

After a moment's hesitation, she pulled him down with her, lying back as he pressed languid kisses to her throat and behind her ear.

"Are you sure?" he murmured.

"Mm-hmm." She brushed her lips over his, tasting wine and desire there. He was exactly what she'd been yearning for, and just for now, she planned to take her fill of him.

Eli rolled onto his side and propped himself up on his elbow. Ribbons of early-morning light peeked through the curtains and painted Sam in hues of orange and gold. She was even prettier while she slept if that was possible. He smoothed an auburn curl off her cheek, and his desire stirred to life, but he didn't have the heart to wake her. He ought to be spent after making love to her three times, yet he wanted her again.

A soft, buzzing noise from the other side of the room pulled his gaze to the chair where he'd left his clothes. There it was again—his cell phone. No one called him this early—except one person, Rodrigo Diaz. He carefully peeled back the covers, slipped out of Sam's bed, and padded across the floor. With a glance at Sam, he left the room to answer the call. Too late to catch it, he checked the display and stiffened when he saw Rodrigo's name.

*Please let him buy my story that Sam doesn't have the sapphire anymore.*

He dialed his voicemail.

"Mr. Kincaid, I would love to believe you," Rodrigo said in the message. "Unfortunately, you've already shown me that you can't be trusted."

Damn it.

Rodrigo went on. "But since today is my fortieth wedding anniversary, I'm in a generous mood. I'll give you another twenty-four hours to report back with an update. Does Miss Cartwright have the sapphire or not? If she does, then it's time to make your move and grab it. I'd hate for any harm to come to Lizzy. Mystic Pines seems like a nice place. I'm sure she'd like to go on living." He laughed. "Go on living *there* was what I meant to say. Or perhaps not."

A chill rolled over Eli's skin. He ended the call, but another message came through right away—a photo that made his blood run cold. He immediately recognized the short, brown, and gray hair, the narrow shoulders. The picture had been taken from behind—probably through a window—and clearly showed his sister in her wheelchair. A time stamp on the bottom of the photo displayed yesterday's date.

H clenched his jaw. Barely able to breathe, he returned to Sam's bedroom. As he dressed, he avoided looking at her. What the hell was he supposed to do, sacrifice his own sister? It was a longshot, but he had to try to get to Lizzy and move her to a different facility—one where Diaz couldn't find her—in the next twenty-four hours. After that was taken care of, he'd tell the slimy loan shark that he was sure Sam didn't have the jewel. And then he'd disappear. It was the only solution he could come up with to keep both Lizzy and Sam from harm. They were both innocent. If anyone should suffer consequences for his actions, that someone had to be him.

With a final glance at Sam, an unbearable heaviness bore down on his chest. On his way out, he glimpsed her portfolio, open on the kitchen table. Her drawing of him had more detail than it had the day before. Had she worked on it during the night as he'd slept? He swallowed past the lump in his throat then slipped out the door.

# Chapter Seven

Sam handed her first customer of the day his purchase—one of her smaller still life paintings. "Thanks so much." She stuck the two hundred-dollar bills into her jeans pocket.

"My wife is going to love this." He took a business card from the holder on the counter. "Don't be surprised if she comes in for more."

The prospect lifted her mood even higher. The only thing that could make her day better would be if Eli came into the store. She'd been disappointed when she woke up alone, but she could hardly expect him to sleep in as late as she had.

After the best sex of her life, she hadn't been able to shut off her mind, so she'd done what she always did when insomnia set in—she'd worked on one of her pieces. The drawing of Eli was nearly finished. Maybe she'd add the last few touches today, and present it to him tonight.

She used the time between customers to shade and shadow the drawing. Just a few more details and it would be done. She texted Eli that she'd have it ready to give him tonight.

At the sound of the door chimed, she glanced up and found the blonde woman from the cat café, Jordan. "Hey, this is from Luna," Jordan explained. "She said you love her cinnamon buns and she has more than she needs for today. I think someone placed a special order for them and then canceled it."

"Wow, that sucks for Luna. But I won't complain." Sam retrieved her wallet to pay for the order, but Jordan shook her head.

"No charge. Luna told me to tell you not to be a stranger." Jordan glanced up at the artwork on the walls. "This is new. These are great."

"Thank you."

"Are they yours?"

"Mm-hmm."

Jordan widened her eyes. "I'm so impressed. Hey, do you ever draw cats?"

"I haven't, although I probably could."

The blonde held her fist over her mouth. "Hmm."

Before Sam could ask what Jordan was thinking, the blonde headed toward the door. "See you tomorrow," she called.

Shaking her head, Sam delved into the bag of pastries and bit into a still-warm cinnamon bun. She managed to eat most of the confection before a customer came in.

The fifty-ish brunette picked up several small bundles of sage and set them on the counter. "Just these, please."

As Sam rang up the woman's purchase, the brunette pointed to one of Sam's portraits. "I love that. How much is that one?"

"Um..." Sam's father had once told her that

when he vended at various gem and mineral shows around the country, he tried to size up any potential buyers before he gave them a price for one of his items. How expensive were their clothes, how refined their speech?

Sam took in the woman's buttery leather designer purse, and her perfectly manicured nails. "Two-fifty," she told the customer.

The woman pursed her red lips. "I'll take it."

"Yes, ma'am." Sam's pulse pounded. She used a step ladder to retrieve the portrait then rolled it and tied it with green ribbon. The moment the customer left, Sam let out the cheer she'd been holding back. She couldn't wait to share the news that she'd sold a painting with Eli, but she didn't want to text or call him again since she'd already left him a message earlier.

A group of three women arrived at the shop and started browsing. Minutes later, a man as big as a linebacker, dressed all in black, entered while the women were still shopping. He stood at the bookshelf and flipped through several of the herb books. After Sam had rung up the women's purchases, they left, leaving only the man.

Outside, clouds darkened the sky. Thunder boomed in the distance. "We could use that rain, hmm?"

He gave her a tight smile, and she noticed a long L-shaped scar across his cheek.

"Can I help you find something?" she asked him.

He returned the book to the shelf. Staring toward one of the paintings, he shrugged. "Maybe. I like that."

She followed his gaze to the piece she'd done of her father.

"What's that in his hand?" He stepped closer to the painting and narrowed his eyes toward it.

"A brooch." Something about him made her nervous. She wished Eli was there. Goosebumps rose on her skin. She moved behind the counter. Opening the drawer where her aunt kept the knife a few inches, she reached her hand inside and felt around for the weapon. Her fingers touched the cool metal.

"What's the significance of the that?" the man asked. His suit was expensive, judging by the rich-looking fabric and how well it fit. He didn't seem like the sort of person who'd rob a store. A high-end jewelry store or a bank maybe…

When he cut his eyes at her and raised his brow, she remembered that she hadn't answered his last question. Something niggled at her insides. She didn't want the guy to know a darn thing about her, or about the brooch. She coughed. "Oh, um…I just goofed a spot there and decided to cover it. No significance, just an oops."

He nodded slowly as if he wasn't quite sure he believed her. Then without another word, he left.

Relief swept through her. She exhaled the breath she hadn't realized she'd been holding then checked the time on her cell. 5:30 and still no response from Eli. Her shaky confidence faltered. Would he disappear now that she'd slept with him? Was he destined to be yet another scar on her heart?

Not that she'd changed her mind about not wanting more than a no-strings fling with him. So what that in the few days since he'd entered her life he'd done more for her than guys who'd hung around for weeks. Didn't matter that he seemed to care.

Ignoring the thick clog in her throat, she straightened up the bookshelf, then cleaned the glass display cases and counter. Movement out front caught her eye. The big guy in the fancy suit stood near the fountain in the courtyard, speaking into his phone. He kept glancing toward the shop.

Something about him bothered her, but she couldn't put her finger on what exactly it was.

The cat café, the beauty salon, and the yoga studio were closed now. Only Medici, the Italian restaurant across the courtyard was still open. Sam locked the front door and checked her cell again. Still, no messages or texts. Last thing she wanted to do was keep bugging Eli.

*Needy is unattractive.*

Her mom used to tell her that every time Sam asked her for anything.

Why was that weird guy still hanging around?

She could call the sheriff's office, but what would she say? That some dude was giving her the creeps? Surely, she was overreacting. By the time she finished getting the store ready to close, the man would probably be gone. But after a few minutes, he was still out there, no longer on his phone, now sitting at one of the bistro tables, staring toward Eye of Newt. And now it was getting dark outside as a storm rolled in.

She turned off the lights and watched the man from behind the bookshelf. After another glance toward the shop, he walked away. Sam drew a relieved breath. She waited a few minutes before leaving the store and heading to her car. Before she came to the end of Calico Court, she noticed the same man hanging around her Impala.

He strode past it then sat on a nearby bench. Did he know that was her car?

A shiver of fear rolled over her skin as she ducked into a shadow between the buildings. Swallowing hard, she dialed Eli's number. To heck with not wanting to seem needy.

Eli's recorded message told her to leave a message.

"Hey, it's me, Sam. If you're anywhere near the herb shop, would you mind coming by? There's this creepoid guy outside, and…" She huffed. "It's probably nothing. I'm hesitant to call the cops. I mean, he's not doing anything except not leaving, but he's making me nervous."

Scanning the area after she hung up, she didn't see the guy anymore. She released a big breath, and with it a bit of her anxiety. Until he came around a dark SUV parked a few yards away. He looked right at her as he lit a cigarette before climbing into the SUV.

No way was she going to get into the Impala now. Why let him know that it was hers? She stashed her cell in her purse and returned to the store, locking herself inside. If she waited a few minutes, surely the man would move on. Sitting on the stool behind the counter, she checked her phone for messages.

A noise pulled her attention toward the front of the store. Someone was jiggling the door handle. Her mouth went dry. The scary guy stood at the door, his hands cupped over the glass as he looked inside. Sam's blood ran cold.

Alarm bucked through Eli. He floored the accelerator. He'd just crossed the county line on his way out of town when he'd played Sam's message. Making an illegal U-turn to get to her, he gripped the steering wheel with sweaty hands and muttered a curse under his breath.

Had to be one of Diaz's henchmen at Eye of Newt. How many thugs worked for Diaz? One had been in Atlanta only yesterday, close enough to Lizzy to take her picture. Eli had called Mystic Pines early in the morning to make arrangements for his sister to be moved to a different facility. God willing, that would keep her safe. He'd hoped to be there for the move, but at the moment, Sam needed him more.

He'd taken Diaz at his word that he'd give Eli a day to ascertain if Sam had the sapphire. Why would he think the loan shark could be trusted? The man was a criminal, after all. Now Sam might be in danger, and it was all his fault. He offered up a silent prayer that the person Sam had described wasn't one of Rodrigo's goons, and that whoever it was didn't have nefarious intentions.

Passing the welcome sign to Cat's Paw Cove, Eli's pulse sped up. Almost there. When he turned onto Sherwood Boulevard, a dark SUV with heavily tinted windows passed him going the other way. The driver was impossible to make out, but the hair on the back of Eli's neck stood on end.

Swallowing past the acid in the back of his throat, he drove as fast he dared through town. He parked on Whiskers Lane then ran into the courtyard to the herb shop and banged on the door. The place was locked, and the lights were out.

*Please let Sam be okay.*

Thankfully, she came to the door and let him inside.

Eli blew out a deep breath, and with it, some of his worry. "Are you all right?" he asked.

"Sure, fine." But her wide eyes betrayed her assurances.

"Tell me the truth."

The pulse at her temples fluttered. "I got scared when the guy tried the door handle. I didn't let him in, of course. When I took out my phone and acted like I was calling the cops, he left."

Eli pulled her against him, smoothing down her unruly hair. "You had me worried." He kissed the top of her head. "Come on. Let's get out of here." Grabbing her art supplies, he went ahead of her and waited for her to lock up. Everything seemed copasetic on the street.

He checked Sam's car then stashed her things in the back seat. "Are you going to your aunt's house?"

She nodded. "Want to come over?"

More than she knew. But he needed to check on his sister. He had a friend in Atlanta he hoped would be able to drop in on Lizzy for a visit. No telling how she'd do with a sudden move to a new facility. Since he wasn't able to travel to Atlanta right away, phone calls to the key staff members would have to suffice, and that would take some research. "How about later this evening?"

Sam narrowed her eyes at him.

"I have a couple things to take care of first."

Shrugging, she started her car. "Okay. See you later then."

"Be aware of your surroundings, okay?"

"I will." Her lips bunched to one side. "Are you all right? You seem…I don't know, nervous."

He scrubbed a hand over his face. "I'm just concerned about you, that's all."

"Thanks for rescuing me."

His chest tightened. Had he brought this danger into her life? Although Diaz might have sent someone way scarier after her if Eli hadn't screwed up and been assigned the task of getting her sapphire. Maybe he was fooling himself, rationalizing away blame that rested squarely upon his shoulders. "I'll see you soon." He shut her car door then waited as she pulled away from the curb.

Rescuing her? If she only knew.

Sam braked to let a pair of blondes cross the road in front of her. Wait, she knew that woman. And the other one—it was Jordan and Mallory, the twins from the cat café and the salon, respectively. One of them appeared to be searching for something. The blonde in the black shirt dashed ahead of her sister into a cloche of trees on the edge of the Sherwood House grounds.

The other twin shook her head and followed.

Something about the situation made Sam think that the twins were in trouble or at least upset. Sam parked her car and headed after them. "Hey," she called to the closer one. "Are you guys okay?"

The blonde narrowed her eyes at Sam for a moment then gave her a tight smile and closed the distance between them. "Jordan does this all the time."

Her statement only clarified that Sam was

speaking to Mallory. "Does what?" Sam asked her. "Is she all right? I just saw her a little while ago."

Mallory gestured at side-by-side tree stumps and sat on one of them.

Sam joined her.

"My sister talks to animals," Mallory said.

Sam shrugged. "I do, too. I spoke to my aunt's cat, Ginger just this morning."

Mallory shook her head. "You don't understand. Jordan telepathically communicates with cats, dogs, birds, horses, all sorts of animals."

"Oh, I see." For someone who had a ton of relatives with various forms of magic, Sam didn't have trouble believing Mallory's claim. "Can you?" she asked. "I mean, you two are identical, right?"

"We are, but we have different gifts. Tarot cards are my gift, as you saw."

Jordan's disembodied voice interrupted their conversation. "Do you have a home? Oh, I see."

Mallory rolled her eyes. "Everywhere she goes, she finds a stray, and sometimes she convinces it to let her take it to the cat café or the local animal shelter."

"I see," Sam said.

"Do you live at the Sherwood House?" Jordan said from a few yards away.

Mallory sighed. "I'll probably be here a while. You don't need to stay. We'll be fine."

But Sam didn't feel comfortable leaving Mallory sitting in the dark with her twin wandering about in the heavily wooded park. "It's fine," Sam said. "I've got time."

Mallory opened her purse and took out a small fabric-wrapped bundle. She peeled away the cloth to reveal a deck of tarot cards. "Want a quick reading? My sixth sense is telling me that you had unresolved questions from the last one I did for you."

Sam realized that the psychic's prediction about a whirlwind romance had come true. But Mallory had also said something about the guy not being trustworthy. Sam's stomach suddenly ached. "Um…sure. If you don't mind."

"Not at all." Mallory handed her the deck. "Try to concentrate on your question as you shuffle."

As Sam shuffled, she concentrated on Eli and their new relationship. Yes, even though they'd just met, and Sam hesitated to form any attachments, she felt a connection to Eli that she didn't want to lose. But was being with Eli a mistake? She handed the cards back to Mallory.

Mallory stood up and fanned them out on the tree stump. "Pick three." After Sam chose her cards, Mallory shined her cell phone's flashlight down on them and grimaced. Touching a card with a scary-looking man on it, she pursed her lips. "You—or someone you're close to—is entrapped by a man, attached to him by use of trickery. The Devil is a complicated card, though. Along with these others in the spread, it could mean a strong sexual connection as well."

Sam gulped. Was Eli somehow tricking her?

"I see someone either with a lot of wealth, physical strength, or a great deal of erotic power." The psychic stared at the cards for several more moments. "I have to be honest. This is a warning. You see how the three swords pierce a heart?"

Dread settled deep in Sam's bones. "Yes. That doesn't look promising."

"And with the seven of swords, there's probably some sneakiness involved. This man has an agenda and might mean you harm. Does this make sense in your life?"

Gulping, she nodded. "It does," she managed. Again she'd thrown caution to the wind and allowed herself to be taken in by someone who wasn't good for her. "And it's so similar to the reading you gave me a few days ago."

Mallory gathered up the cards and wrapped them in the cloth, her face solemn. "You know, this is open to interpretation. Never assume that you can't change the road you're on. The tarot merely tells us the path we're traveling at the moment, and sometimes the consequences of the choices we make. There's nothing to stop you from changing your destiny."

Nothing to stop her from ending things with Eli—nothing but her heart. She should never have let him in there. Only she had. She'd broken her own rule of only engaging in casual flings. How had she allowed herself to start caring about Eli so quickly?

Jordan stepped out from behind some hibiscus bushes. "Oh, hi, Sam. What are you doing here?"

"I was driving home and saw you and Mallory," she explained. "You looked as if you might need help."

"Aw, thank you. That's so sweet." Jordan hugged her. "I saw a cat who looked scared. I went after him to see if he was okay."

"And?" Mallory asked.

Jordan smiled at her twin. "He lives near here, but he comes to the Sherwood House to play with some of the Sherwood cats."

Mallory furrowed her brow. "The Sherwood cats?"

"There are dozens of cats that live on the grounds," Jordan explained to her sister.

Sam nodded. "Legend has it that they're all descended from the original mousers that traveled here from England on the ship that sank in the harbor. Aunt Emma says that all the Sherwood cats are magic."

"That's true," Jordan said. "Hey, Sam, Mallory and I were headed to The Galley for dinner. They've got great Scotch eggs and fish and chips. And we always play darts after we eat. Want to join us? I'll warn you, though. My sister is super competitive, and she usually wins."

Sam remembered that she was supposed to be meeting Eli at the cottage. But now that she'd had a second reading warning her about him, she wasn't so sure she should spend any more time with him. She needed a little while to process her thoughts. "I appreciate it, and if it's okay, I'll take a raincheck."

"Of course," Mallory said. "Have a good night."

"You, too." Instead of going home, she made a U-turn and drove toward her favorite spot in town—a hill overlooking the harbor where, as a kid, she'd spent hours sketching and painting.

She needed to draw and think. As much as she liked Eli, she wasn't ready to face him.

# Chapter Eight

Where the hell was Sam? Eli had watched her drive away from the store with his own eyes more than an hour ago. She should have arrived at her aunt's cottage five minutes later, but she obviously hadn't since her car wasn't there. Could someone have intercepted her? Dread roiled in his belly as he knocked on the door to the cottage again.

Lightning lit up the sky, quickly followed by a boom of thunder. Why hadn't he gone with his gut and followed that SUV he'd seen earlier? What if Diaz's man had Sam? He tried her cell but went straight to her voicemail. "Please call me, Sam. I'm worried. Where are you?" Gritting his teeth, he disconnected and paced the small mulch-covered parking pad. The nearest neighbor was at least thirty yards away, and considering the dense cloche of trees between the homes, someone could have dragged a person out of the cottage kicking and screaming, and no one would be the wiser.

He flashed on the faces of those sons of bitches who'd roughed him up in Atlantic City. They could have kidnapped Sam, then taken her somewhere else to persuade her to tell them where the sapphire was. What if they'd followed her here and hurt her. God, the notion cut through him like jagged glass.

He returned to the front door and tried the handle. Locked. Next, he checked the front windows, but they didn't budge. As he was about to walk away, something moved inside one of the windows. Heart racing, he realized it was merely Sam's aunt's cat. "Where is Sam, Ginger?" he asked the feline.

Ginger stretched against the glass.

"You're no help at all," Eli told the animal as he continued to the next window.

Around the side of the house, he found an unlocked one and easily slipped it open just as the cloudburst hit. He climbed through into Sam's bedroom, landing on the dresser.

The cat jumped onto Sam's nightstand and meowed. If only the animal really could tell him something.

A quick search of the cottage yielded no clues as to Sam's whereabouts. At least there was no sign of any kind of a struggle. He allowed himself a modicum of relief. Didn't appear that she'd been there yet. Maybe she'd changed her mind about going home and had instead gone to the grocery store or the gas station. But the ease with which he'd been able to gain access to the house didn't bode well for her safety, should anyone come after her.

After checking that the rest of the windows in the cottage were locked, he returned to Sam's room and tried to lock the one he'd entered, but the latch was just out of reach. As he climbed onto the dresser to get closer, his foot slipped and knocked off a ceramic vase. The loud crash in the silent house stopped him cold.

Damn it. Now Sam would know someone had been there. Muttering a curse, he turned on his phone's flashlight and started picking up the broken fragments. His gaze landed on a small drawstring pouch in the middle of the shards of pottery. He dusted it off and felt something rigid inside.

Could it be…? With trembling fingers, he loosened the string and fished out a sapphire brooch. God, he could barely breathe. The gem warmed in his palm. It was beautiful—even more dazzling than the matching one Rodrigo had shown him.

What the hell was he supposed to do now? Sam believed that the jewelry was the key to her future, so how could he rob her of that? Unless… Maybe by merely possessing the piece, her future—her very life—was in jeopardy. If he called Rodrigo and told him he'd located the jewel and was on his way to deliver it, the mobster would call off his goons, and Sam would be safe. Yes, that's what he'd do.

An unseen vise clamped down hard on his chest. Sam was going to be destroyed to find the sapphire gone, especially if she figured out that he'd taken it. He didn't have a choice, though—he had to keep her out of harm's way.

He did his best to hide the ceramic fragments under the dresser then forced the lock on the window. On his way out, he hesitated a moment, inhaled her scent, which still lingered in the house. Much as it devastated him to know he'd never see her again, that was his only option—the only way to know she'd be all right, at least physically. She'd be heartbroken to learn that he'd taken the brooch, but at least she'd be alive.

He left through the front door, making sure it was secure as he did. Dodging raindrops, he ran to his car. "Goodbye, Sam." Clamping down on his emotions, he hurried away.

Sam parked in front of the cottage. Usually, drawing made her feel a little better when she was down. Not this time. She'd spent nearly half an hour on her favorite hill with her sketchpad, but she'd only wasted several sheets on dismal pencil drawings that looked as if a kid had made them. Besides, it had started storming shortly after she'd gotten to her spot, and drawing in the rain was impossible.

At least she didn't have to face Eli yet. She'd shut off her phone in case he called. She just wasn't ready to see him yet. The tarot readings had been pretty clear.

Inside the house, she went to her room to change out of her wet clothes, and breathed in the hint of a pleasant scent, something familiar, like the beach.

Ginger was curled up in the middle of Sam's bed. She looked up at Sam and trilled.

"I'll feed you in a minute, kitty." As she slipped on a pair of sweatpants, an uneasy feeling settled in her gut. The wind howled outside and slammed branches against the roof. She strode to the window and pulled the curtains closed. A dark oval-shaped stain in the center of the dresser scarf caught her eye. Aunt Emma had put a vase there years ago to hide the spot—the vase where Sam had hidden the brooch. Her breath locked. A quick scan of the room confirmed that the vase was missing, but nothing else appeared to be gone. It had definitely been there in the morning. Before she'd left, she'd moved it aside to close the window.

*Please, no.*

The sapphire could have given her a future. She was sure that was why her father had willed it to her. Nausea swirled in her gut.

Sniffing the air again, she realized what she smelled—Eli's cologne. He'd been there, and more recently than in the wee hours of the morning. A heavy weight pressed her chest.

What if the thief was still in the house? She couldn't pin Eli's name to that role, not without more information. She hated to even consider that he'd broken into Aunt Emma's house, but in light of both tarot readings, and the fact that the vase was missing, who else could it have been?

Pulse hammering at her temples, she padded to the kitchen, grabbed a knife and searched the entire cottage. At least the burglar was gone. She returned to her bedroom with the weapon, just in case. A jagged chunk of pottery stuck out from under the dresser. She got on her hands and knees and found more—lots more. After she'd gathered all the fragments, she felt around for the pouch that held her sapphire, but it was gone.

Eli.

She sat against the dresser and buried her face in her hands. Why had she let a virtual stranger into her life? Looking back over the last few days, she should have known he'd been too good to be true. He'd showed up at exactly the right moment and had immediately started charming her with his offers of help, and his good looks. Again, she'd let her heart overrule her head. Now she'd lost the only thing of value she'd ever owned, the very item her aunt had said was so vital to her future.

Damn it. Was she destined to continue making stupid, self-destructive choices the rest of her life? She strode to the bed and opened her portfolio to her drawing of Eli, clenching her teeth to hold back tears.

Where had he come from? How had he learned where she'd hidden the sapphire? Had he been watching her for a while? Following her? Or had she been her own undoing by telling him about the jewel?

She studied the picture as if it would give up his secrets, and provide her with the answers she sought. Unwanted images of the two of them locked in passion filled her head. He'd touched her so tenderly. She'd yearned to believe he was different from the others. He was, she supposed. Rather than merely using her for sex, he'd manipulated her with it.

Sinking onto the mattress, she let the sadness linger, the latest betrayal in her life. She tore the drawing in half, destroying it just as Eli had wrecked her heart. Then she crinkled the pieces, and closed her eyes, finally giving in to tears.

She prayed for sleep's release, only it refused to come. Tossing and turning, she couldn't escape the sound of his voice, the scent of his skin. She closed her eyes for what seemed like the hundredth time that night.

Lightning flared blue through the curtains. A crack of thunder shook the house. Then the distinctive crash of breaking glass.

Sam bolted upright, suddenly wide awake. Her heartbeat drummed in her ears. More glass shattered. Grabbing fistfuls of the bedsheets, she listened.

The wind had died down. Something clicked—a door lock, a gun?

Afraid to breathe, she tried to focus on the door in the dark. Another flash of lightning illuminated the room. The knife she'd carried into her room earlier was stiff on the dresser, only a few steps away. But would the creaky wood floor give her away?

Her fingers trembled as she eased back the covers, grabbing her cell as she did. With another glance at the doorknob, she tiptoed to the dresser and picked up the knife.

A million scenarios raced through her brain—a stranger was in the house; it was a prowler, who'd leave when he heard her; or perhaps Eli had returned to silence her.

No, Eli wouldn't—couldn't hurt her. And he already had the only thing of value she'd owned, didn't he? Then she remembered that the creepy guy at the store today had asked about the jewel in the painting. But how could he know she had it? Unless—

The floorboards outside her room creaked. A metallic click followed and amped up her terror. With a death grip on her weapon, she stepped away from the window and into the shadows behind the chair. She crouched and offered up a silent plea that whoever was on the other side of the door meant her no harm.

With a sweaty hand, she tapped a button to wake her phone. The indigo light of the screen seemed so much brighter in the dark. If she phoned the police, the intruder would surely hear her. So she texted Eli a single word—"Help."

Her door opened, only a crack. She squeezed her eyes closed and held her breath. Footfalls receded. Another door opened somewhere. But just when she was praying the burglar would leave, her door opened wider.

"Sam?" someone whispered. Footsteps came closer.

Eli? She couldn't tell, only that it was a man.

Hot-cold shivers racked her body. She didn't dare peek around the chair to see him.

Suddenly he shoved the chair aside and grabbed her from behind, hauling her up against a solid wall of muscle and pinning her left arm between them.

She screamed, only for the second it took for him to cover her mouth. Before she could stab him with the knife, he'd immobilized her right arm. She struggled but knew it was useless. God, he was so strong. She tasted his leather glove as he tightened his grip on her. The knife slipped from her hand, clanging to the floor.

*I won't die like this.*

She bit down on his finger. Growling, he crushed his hand against her neck, cutting off her air supply.

"Where's the sapphire brooch?" he ground out.

Panic mixed with a kernel of relief that it

wasn't Eli.

"Where?" he shouted.

She tried to speak, but her voice came out a croak. When he loosened his hold a little, she kicked him and lunged toward the knife.

Before she could get it, he lifted her off the floor and bashed her head against the wall, hard. Dizziness and nausea drained all the fight from her.

Lightning gave her the briefest glimpse of his face—the L-shaped scar crossing his cheek. It was the man who'd been hanging around the parking lot. Why hadn't she listened to her instincts and called the cops?

"Tell me where the damn sapphire is, bitch!"

"I don't know," she managed.

A punch to her stomach knocked the wind out of her. She doubled over, gasping.

He grabbed a handful of her hair and twisted it, pulling so forcefully that she couldn't help but scream.

"Tell me."

"Someone…stole it."

Pain exploded at the base of her skull. All she could see was blackness as she fought to hang on to consciousness. If she let go, she knew she'd never wake. But the haze crept through her head in a moment. And everything went dark.

Something was wrong. Eli had been expecting an angry phone call from Sam as soon as she'd discovered the brooch was missing, but her one-word text frightened the hell out of him. Had he made a mistake with the gem? Too late now. He'd pushed the locker key under the door of Sam's aunt's store a moment before her text came through.

Muttering a curse, he ran to his car and headed toward the cottage. The storm made for lousy visibility, but he drove along the twisting roads as fast as he dared. When he got there, none of the lights were on. Even the nearby cottages were dark. The storm must have knocked out power.

He used his cell's flashlight to find his way. His dread grew at the sight of wide, deep tire tracks in the wet ground a few yards from Sam's car.

*The SUV I saw earlier.*

He banged on the door to the cottage before trying the handle. It was open, and the place was a mess. Cabinets, closets, and drawers were open, the contents littering the counters and the floor. Every nerve and muscle shifted to high alert as he tore through the house, room by room, in search of Sam. She had to be all right. "Sam? Are you okay?"

Silence.

When he entered her bedroom, his light found a dark streak on the wall. The hair on his nape stood on end.

*Blood. Sam's blood.*

Panic drummed in his ears. He crossed the room in a few steps. Sam lay in a heap on the floor.

*Please let her be alive.*

Her weak moan sparked his hope. He lifted her into his arms and gently set her down on the bed.

She whimpered and hugged her arms over her stomach.

Giving her a quick once-over with his light, he shuddered. Her only visible injury was a gash on her forehead. He grabbed a shirt from an open drawer to apply pressure to the wound then called 911. That done, he cradled her in his arms, offering up a silent prayer that the paramedics would hurry.

A lamp on the nightstand flickered a couple times before coming back on. The mechanical hum of the air conditioner filled the quiet.

Sam stirred, blinked against the light.

"The paramedics will be here soon." He swallowed. "And the police."

The hurt in her eyes was worse than he could have imagined as she looked up at him. "You took my brooch, didn't you?"

A thousand-pound weight compressed his chest. Clenching his jaw, he averted his gaze and nodded.

Tears rolled over her cheeks. "How could you? Give it back."

"I don't have it, Sam. It's in a locker at the bus station in town. I slipped the key under the door to your aunt's shop. The envelope has the locker number written on the inside flap."

When Sam furrowed her brow in confusion, he took a deep breath. Then he explained how he'd come to find her, about his gambling debt and Rodrigo's henchmen roughing him up, and threatening his sister. "I never expected that I'd start caring about you, and I knew I couldn't betray you. I hoped that I could protect both you and my sister. I've moved Lizzy to a safer facility. As for me…" He straightened. "I'm going to confess to the police. It's the only way to stop Diaz, and protect you and my sister for good."

He expected Sam to turn away in disgust, to

yell at him, or tell him to get the hell out. Instead, she grasped his hand. “Don’t tell the cops anything, not yet.”

Shaking his head, he smoothed her hair off her face and checked her cut. Thankfully the bleeding had stopped, although she’d probably need stitches. “I have to. Rodrigo Diaz needs to be locked up.”

Sirens sounded in the distance, growing louder by the second.

Her tears started flowing again, and the sight broke him. “I don’t want you to go to jail, and you will if you confess to stealing the sapphire.” She squeezed his arm. “Leave now, before the police show up. I’ll be fine.”

“Not until I know you’re safe.” No way in hell was he going to leave her alone.

Colored lights flashed through the curtains.

Sam tried to sit up but winced. “I’ll tell them the guy who did this to me was the one who stole the sapphire.”

“Time for me to man up.” He pressed a kiss to the back of her hand. “I’ve never met anyone like you before. I’ll understand if, after the dust has settled, you want nothing more to do with me. But you have to know, you’re an incredible woman, Sam—beautiful, talented and smart.”

She started to shake her head, but he stopped her with a kiss. “You are smart. More than that—you’re wise, and you’ve got such a kind heart.” Leaving her, he went to the door to let in the emergency personnel.

The next half hour was a blur of uniformed men and women tromping through the cottage, tending to Sam, questioning him, and finally saying goodbye to her. As long as she was safe, and Lizzy was, too, he'd deal with whatever consequences he had to.

# Chapter Nine

Five days after that awful night at the cottage, Sam helped a customer find geranium essential oil. "Thanks," the customer said when Sam handed her the bag. "I hope your day gets better."

"Hmm?"

The brunette shrugged. "You seem so sad. Whatever it is, I'm sure it'll be okay."

Pasting on a smile, Sam stood up taller. "Thanks, I'm fine."

After the woman left, Sam headed to the back room. Despite several attempts to draw over the past few days, she'd been unable to complete even the simplest sketch. Her muse refused to join her.

If only she could get Eli off her mind. He hadn't called, and she was beginning to think she might never hear from him again. It was probably for the best, but she couldn't shake the emptiness his absence had left inside her.

When the front door chimed, she returned to the main room to find her Aunt Emma. Sam closed the distance between them and wrapped her arms as far around her aunt as they'd reach. Breathing in the comforting lavender scent Emma had always worn, Sam hung on for several seconds.

Emma held her at arms' length and looked her over from head to toe. "You're too skinny, child. We'll have to fix that starting tonight. And what's that bandage on your forehead?"

"I'll explain later." Sam ran a finger over the spot. "I've missed you. I hope you had a good time on your cruise."

Her aunt merely raised an eyebrow, her deep blue eyes sparkling mysteriously. "I hope you can forgive me for throwing you to the wolves here. Looks like you've managed fine at the store." She sighed. "I need to sit down. We've had a long drive from Port Canaveral."

We? Sam relieved Emma of the heavy purse she carried. "I'll turn the closed sign around. It's almost lunchtime anyway. Do you want to go get something to eat?"

Aunt Emma shook her head. "Let's speak here, in private. Go ahead and lock up, though. I don't want any interruptions."

Sam did as she asked then grabbed a couple Moon Pies and joined Emma at the table in back, handing the older woman one of the snacks. "Are you going to tell me why you've kept me hanging about the sapphire?"

Emma took a bite of her Moon Pie and nodded. After she swallowed, she opened her purse and took out her oracle cards, the same deck Sam had seen her use hundreds of times. "You know I do readings for you, even when you're not here. I do that so I can warn you if I see something bad or dangerous in your path."

"I figured that." Sam sat on the edge of her seat. Her aunt's advice was what she'd been waiting for.

Finishing the sweet, Emma pulled a wadded-up tissue from her purse to wipe her fingers. "Before I get into the reason I told you to hold onto the brooch your father left you, I want to apologize for dumping all this…" She waved her hand through the air. "…on your shoulders. I suppose I was caught up in the moment. You see, I met someone, on the internet. It was Phillip's idea to take a cruise. He bought the tickets to surprise me. When I realized we were to set sail the very day you were planning to arrive, I almost canceled. But instead, I did a reading."

What? Emma had a boyfriend? She'd been single Sam's whole life, or at least, that's what Sam had always assumed. "O-okay."

"The cards said that it was vitally important that you not part with the jewel—not yet, anyway." She smoothed a lock of salt-and-pepper hair off her forehead. "My sources on the other side told that the sapphire was going to give you the push you needed to move past all the hurdles holding you back from living your life. You were stuck in a rut, I think. That magical brooch was crucial to the transition."

Sam had to agree with that. And in a roundabout way, the jewel had been a vehicle of sorts, one that had led her to open her heart to someone, which she'd been so terrified to do. Until she'd started falling for Eli. Even though she might never see him again, she'd never forget him. Over another Moon Pie, she filled Emma in on all the drama and intrigue that had unfolded in her absence.

Emma listened intently. After Sam had finished her story, her aunt set her hand over the deck of cards. "I did another reading for you this morning before we got off the ship. The message has changed."

Sam set down her Moon Pie. "Oh?"

"The time is right to let go of the treasure you hold."

"So I'm supposed to sell it now?" Sam asked.

Emma shook her head. "It was never truly yours. You were merely holding it for a while."

Sam struggled to understand what her aunt meant. "What? After all, I've been through you think I should just hand over the sapphire to someone?"

"Not exactly. The message will become clearer in the coming days." Aunt Emma's head lolled to one side for a moment. "Pardon me. I'm so tired after the trip. I'm going to close my eyes for a few minutes."

"Sure," Sam said. "Go ahead."

Someone knocked at the door, so Sam headed to the front room.

A tall, middle-aged blonde pointed to Sam's artwork. "Are you the artist?" she called through the glass.

At the opportunity to possibly sell a drawing or painting, Sam unlocked the door and let the woman in. "Yes, I'm Samantha Cartwright."

The woman shook hands with her. "It's a pleasure to meet you. My name's Angie." She tipped her chin toward the painting of Sam's dad. "So that's it, hmm? The missing sapphire brooch."

Sam froze. How'd she known about the jewel?

Angie took a step toward Sam and lowered

her voice. "I'm sorry. I didn't mean to frighten you. Let me explain. I read a news article about the brooch that was seized from a mobster in Atlantic City. Fascinating story about how a case here led them to that awful man and his collection of stolen antique items. I'm a curator for the art museum in St. Augustine. We have a collection of antique amulets and talismans. The story piqued my curiosity, so I researched the one the article mentioned. It sounds like quite an interesting piece."

Sam remained silent. She still didn't understand how Angie had found her since the DA's office had promised not to release her name to the public.

"Many times, art objects that are seized during a criminal investigation are later auctioned off to the public. I wanted to make sure the museum got first dibs. So I contacted the DA here. She told me that the brooch belonged to an artist whose work is on display at a store in Cat's Paw Cove. You have no idea how many shops I checked out before finding this one—and your artwork."

Aunt Emma let out a loud snore. Sam cleared her throat. "Sorry, my aunt is…resting in the back room."

Angie waved off Sam's apology. "Curators are often detectives, hunting down long-lost treasures, following trails that may or may not lead to a forgotten master's work." The blonde looked up at the painting again. "Boy, did I luck out. Not only has my curiosity about the missing brooch been satisfied, but I think I might have found a very promising new artist."

Sam swallowed. "Really?"

Angie nodded. "You've got a lot of talent."

No, she refused to believe anything a stranger told her. Being naïve and taking people at face value had cost her too much. "Do you have a business card?"

"Sure." She reached into her designer purse, pulled out a card, and handed it to Sam.

*Angela Pierre, Assistant Curator, St. Augustine Museum,* Sam read to herself. Angie appeared to be on the level. A shiver of excitement rolled over Sam's skin. "You really like my work, huh?"

"Absolutely. We have an art study program that's affiliated with the University of Florida."

Sam gasped. Maybe she could handle art school after all. She thought about the sapphire brooch, the only connection she had to her father. But what use could the jewel be to her? Such a special gemstone shouldn't be locked away in a bank. It ought to be somewhere people could admire it.

Having the jewel had made Sam a target. Aunt Emma's words played in Sam's mind. "Let go of the treasure you hold. It was never truly yours." She met Angie's stare. "What does it cost to enroll in your art study program?"

Glancing toward Sam's paintings, Angie smiled. "We have a few scholarships available. With a talent like yours, I'm positive you'll be accepted into the program free of charge."

Sam cheered. "Wow. You made my day."

"About the brooch," Angie went on. "We'd like to acquire it."

"Acquire it?"

Angie nodded. "Our financial officer will want to appraise it before we make you an offer."

"Okay." Could her day get any better?

"Fantastic. I'll have him phone you." She took a business card from the holder on the counter. "And if you'll call me tomorrow, I'll arrange to bring you in for a tour."

Head buzzing, Sam couldn't wait to share the news with Eli. But then she remembered that he was in jail, and her mood clunked. So many thoughts raced through her brain. One thing she was sure of, though—she now knew what she wanted to do with the brooch.

Before she did, though, she was going to use the gem's magic.

Eli pushed his sister's wheelchair under a canopy of bougainvillea in the gardens at the group home where she now lived. "This is even nicer than Mystic Pines. Are they treating you well?"

"Very well," Lizzy said. "And I've made friends with several other residents." With obvious effort she lifted her arm and pointed to a shady spot with a wooden bench. "Let's stop there."

He moved her next to the bench and locked the wheels, sensing she had something important to say. "What's on your mind?"

Her pretty smile and bright green eyes were as warm as they'd always been, despite the ravages MS had inflicted upon her body. "You can talk to me, you know. I don't like it when you hide things."

He'd always hated disappointing her, but she was right. Her mind was as sharp as ever, and she deserved the truth. At least he'd already come clean with her about having been a professional gambler, rather than a traveling sales rep, as he'd told her years ago.

Sitting down, he drew a breath before speaking. "I got into some trouble, Lizzy. After a string of bad luck and poor decisions, I tried to run out on a debt. I should have known better. A loan shark threatened me with…." No point in telling her that she'd been in jeopardy. Knowing his sister, she'd blame herself for his wrongdoing. She'd admitted a long time ago that she already felt guilty because Eli had been supplementing her disability payments so she could have the best care. "Let's just say he gave me a deal I wasn't in a position to refuse—one that involved stealing from an innocent woman."

Lizzy flinched. "Oh, Eli. You didn't!"

"Honestly, I'd planned to do it. Until I got to know Sam and to like her." Explaining what he'd done hadn't gotten any easier with repetition or the passage of time. "I did steal it, but I put it in a safe place where only she could retrieve it. And then I turned myself in."

Her face fell. After a long silence, she spoke. "Will you go to prison?"

Taking her hands, he met her stare. "I spent a week in jail. Then my lawyer cut a deal for me. I'll have to testify against some pretty scary dudes, but in exchange, I got probation. Every time I visit you for the next two years, I'll have to get prior authorization, like I did for this trip. Unfortunately, they only allow me one day, so I'll be heading back to Florida in a couple of hours."

"And the young lady?" Lizzy asked. "Will she forgive you?"

Just the mention of Sam stirred up so many emotions and unresolved issues. "I'm praying she will, but only time will tell."

Sam waved to a young couple as they left after their session with Emma. "Enjoy the rest of your day," Sam said.

Aunt Emma had been back from vacation for a week and a half, and every day she'd had at least five or six readings while Sam took care of customers out front. Even Sam's artwork business had been brisk: she'd sold five of her paintings, but she'd taken one down. She planned to keep the portrait of her father, now that she'd decided to sell the sapphire to the museum.

When her stomach growled, she checked the clock. It was just past one, and the only thing she'd eaten for breakfast was a Moon Pie. "Want lunch, Aunt Emma?" she called.

"Hmm?" her aunt mumbled. Seconds later, she stood in the doorway, yawning and rubbing her eyes. "Sure. Would you pick up something sweet for me from the cafe?" She fished a twenty-dollar bill out of her cleavage and handed it to Sam. "And whatever you'd like."

Even though Aunt Emma tried to treat her to lunch every day, Sam was able to buy her own and had even paid for Emma's a couple of times. "I'll be back in a few minutes," Sam told her.

Luna greeted Sam at the café with a quick hug. "Emma's new man seems sweet. She brought him in for breakfast on Sunday."

"Yeah, I like him. And he makes my aunt happier than I've ever seen her." Sam was thrilled for Aunt Emma, but being around people who were obviously in love made Sam lonelier for Eli. She'd have to face the fact that he was probably gone from her life forever.

As Sam waited for her order, she glanced into the cat playroom and saw Jordan holding a Siamese kitty. The blonde appeared to be having a conversation with the feline. Sam chuckled. "Jordan has quite a way with the cats."

Luna nodded as she rang up Sam's order. Winking at Sam, she said, "Jordan has such a gift for communicating with animals. She's amazing."

She certainly was. The town was chock full of residents with wonderful supernatural gifts—but not Sam.

When Sam returned to the herb shop, she set the food on the table in the back room then strode to the bathroom to wash her hands. The front door chimed while she was in there. Knowing that her aunt was there to handle the customer, Sam took her time.

"I've heard about a couple of the herbal remedies you concocted in my absence," Aunt Emma said from the main room of the store. "Sounds as if you've got a talent for that."

Sam dried her hands. Who was Emma talking to? The only person who'd mixed any herbs and oils while Emma had been away was….

The man chuckled, and Sam froze. Could it be…? Heart tattooing a wild beat, Sam ventured a few feet into the other room.

Eli met her stare, and his expression instantly shifted from friendly to contrite. His Adam's apple slid up and then down his throat. "Sam."

Her feet were lead. A gasp slipped from her lips.

Time ceased to exist. He was at her side, wrapping her in the arms she'd longed for. Touching the small bandage on her forehead, he winced. "Can you ever forgive me?"

Words stuck in her mouth. She nodded and buried her face against Eli's chest, breathing in the scent she'd missed so much. Letting go of him, she went to get her sketchpad and opened it to the new portrait of Eli she'd been working on the past couple of days. "I made this for you."

His brow creased. "It's not the same one as before."

No need to tell him that she'd destroyed that one. "I like this one better."

He narrowed his eyes at it. "I don't know how you do it, but I swear, you've captured…a piece of me in that drawing."

Aunt Emma squeezed Sam's shoulder. "That's her magic."

Sam twisted around to look at her aunt. "What do you mean?"

"We've all got a gift, child. That's yours. You somehow portray the essence of everyone you draw." Emma gave Sam a sweet smile. "You're a lucky young lady to have such a talent."

"I think so, too," Eli said.

Sam swallowed past the lump in her throat. "You mean that?"

Taking her face between his hands, Eli kissed her softly. "I swear I'll never lie to you again."

But there was only one way to be sure.

Centering a hand on his chest, she eased him away then hurried into the back room.

"Where are you going?" he asked.

Her aunt stood next to the safe. Sam hadn't even noticed her leaving the front. Their gazes locked, and Sam knew they'd had the same thought.

Emma opened the safe and handed the pouch containing the sapphire brooch to Sam. "Think carefully, child. And trust your heart."

"I have to be sure." Sam took out the jewel and returned to Eli.

He questioned her with his eyes until she opened her palm and showed him the sapphire, the most vibrant ultramarine she'd ever seen.

"Would you answer a couple questions for me?" she asked him.

"Definitely." Without hesitation, he took the gemstone.

Nervous excitement washed over her. "Were you really forced to steal the sapphire from me?"

"Yes." The pain in his eyes was real, palpable. "I swear to you, Sam—"

Something inside her ached, but that betrayal was in the past. She touched her index finger to his lips, stopping him. "You don't have to. I believe you." Extending her hand for the gem, she waited.

He held the brooch to his heart. "Diaz threatened me. I didn't think I had any other choice but to do what he told me. Hurting you was the last thing I wanted, and I promise you, I'll never betray you again." Tiny muscles around his jaw ticked. "I need you to be sure about me."

She returned the jewelry to the pouch. "I already am."

Scooping her into his embrace, he kissed her with a passion she'd never before experienced.

"I love you, Sam." He cupped her face, rubbing his thumb over her cheek.

"Me, too." There was no doubt in her mind—nor in her heart.

# Epilogue

*Three months later…*

Eli turned into the driveway the house he'd rented in Cat's Paw Cove and smiled when he saw Sam's car was already there. She'd moved in two weeks ago, yet he still had to remind himself at least a dozen times a day that this wasn't a dream. Life was good, and getting better with each moment he spent with her.

The instant he opened the door, wonderful aromas filled the air—curry, ginger, and something he couldn't identify.

Sam stood with her back to him at the stove. "How'd your afternoon go?"

He'd been volunteering at the local nursing home for the past few weeks, and he loved every moment of it. And since he'd moved his sister there last month, he now got to see her even more often. "Really well. Lizzy says hi."

Dropping his keys onto the counter, he moved closer to Sam and wrapped his arms around her. He moved aside her damp hair to kiss the back of her neck and inhaled the scent of her shampoo. "I love it when it's your turn to cook. But I can't decide which smells better—you or the food."

"We're having Indian tonight, a new recipe I found on the internet." She turned around to face him wearing a smile that took his breath away. She grabbed a spoon from the drawer and scooped some vegetables and chicken out of the pan. "Taste this. I thought I'd make it next week when Aunt Emma and Phillip come over for dinner." She blew on the food then fed Eli a bite.

He realized the smell he'd been unable to identify was coconut. "Delicious. Your aunt and Phillip are getting serious." Now that he was working at the herb store, spending hours every day with Emma, he was her new confidante.

Sam nodded. "She called me this afternoon and said something about cutting back her hours at the store soon. Now that she has you running things, she can slow down and do some traveling. She never took any vacations when I was a kid, never had anyone she could trust with the business. I'm so glad that she's finally taking time for herself."

He dropped the spoon into the sink. "Tell me about your day."

"Oh my gosh. I stopped by the cat café after school. Jordan introduced me to this cat." She steepled her fingers. "Will you go there with me tomorrow. I want you to meet him."

"A cat?"

"Not just any cat." She grabbed a piece of paper from the counter and showed him a black and white sketch of a tuxedo cat. "Isn't he gorgeous?"

Eli resisted a chuckle. “I gather that we’ll be adopting him tomorrow?”

Sam giggled. “Only if you like him as much as I do. Jordan said he wants to come live with me.”

“I’ll bet she said that.”

Whacking him with a dishtowel, she huffed. “Jordan knows these things.” Sam gasped. “Oh, I almost forgot.” She padded to the table, picked up a large postcard, and handed it to him. “We’re invited to the gala at the museum for the unveiling of the brooch.”

The photo showed the jewel on a velvet platform. Eli pulled Sam into his arms. “I love that we can visit the brooch any time we want.”

“What I love is that it brought you and me together.”

“I’ve always told you how smart you are. See how you nailed that one?” He threaded his fingers through her hair and reeled her in for another kiss. The sapphire’s magic might be all about honesty, but for him, the jewel had transformed his life and brought him to the woman of his dreams.

Want more from Cat's Paw Cove? Turn the page to read an excerpt from Catherine Kean's next book, *Hot Magic*. Releases November 19

While clearing out her late mother's home in Cat's Paw Cove, Florida, Molly Hendrickson finds an unusual antique necklace. Wearing it makes her feel confident and sexy—things she hasn't felt since her ex broke off their engagement or, really, ever. She decides to keep the jewel but takes other items to Black Cat Antiquities, the local antique store, to have them appraised.

Lucian Lord, a reincarnated 12th century knight, moved to Cat's Paw Cove after a scandal in which he revealed his magical abilities to his former girlfriend. Demoted by his superiors, he's running the antiques shop while his grandfather is on vacation. But, when Molly brings in artifacts tainted by dark magic, Lucian is duty-bound to find and contain the dangerous energy before it wreaks havoc not only on the town, but the world.

Living by the knightly code of honor, Lucian vows to help Molly, especially when he realizes the necklace is the source of the ancient magic he's hunting. He's determined to save his headstrong damsel and redeem his tarnished reputation—but first, things will get very, very hot.

Available in eBook and print.

# Chapter One

*Cat's Paw Cove, Florida*
*July, Present Day*

"I *wish* that woman would stop moaning."

In the midst of hanging a gilt-framed watercolor on the wall of Black Cat Antiquities, Lucian Lord glanced at the long-haired, orange and white cat sitting nearby—the feline who'd just spoken in a refined British accent.

"The Lady of the Plate can't help it, Galahad," Lucian said, as the feline jumped up onto the upholstered seat of a Victorian chair. The plaintive moan, coming from the shelf of porcelain plates at the back of the store, started up again. "Remember what my grandfather told us?"

Galahad huffed. "Yeah, yeah, she cries when there's a change in barometric pressure."

"Yes, and—"

"Since it's summer in Florida and the rainy season, she'll likely be wailing a lot. Lucky us."

Lucian fought not to smile. So, Galahad *had* been listening to the conversation, even though at the time he'd been wild-eyed and attacking a pink toy mouse filled with catnip.

"We should have been smart and gone on that cruise with your grandfather and his lady friend. But, no. You agreed to mind the shop. How bloody chivalrous of you."

Lucian returned his attention to the painting. As Galahad well knew, Lucian had agreed to look after the store because he owed his grandfather, and not just for his help with Lucian's recent work crisis. The man had taken twelve-year-old Lucian in and raised him after the horrific car accident in which his parents had died.

Galahad excelled at complaining, but to be fair, he hadn't always been a cat. In truth, he was a reincarnated thirteenth-century squire, a lord's heir, whose ancestors had hailed from Nottinghamshire, England.

Hard to believe some days—not just the reincarnation part, but that Galahad was in fact fifteen years old and not four.

"If I had known about the Lady of the Plate, I might have stayed in Boston," Galahad groused. "I would never have moved with you to this humid, alligator-infested, mosquito-breeding swampland."

"That's not a fair description of Cat's Paw Cove."

"Alligators do live in the lake down the road. Your grandfather said so."

"He did." Lucian straightened the painting.

"And the mosquitoes—"

"And the Sherwood cats." Lucian stole a

glance at Galahad. "You got quite excited about meeting female kitties who have ancestral ties to Nottinghamshire, as you do."

Galahad growled.

Lucian grinned. "Admit it, you were as intrigued to start afresh here as I was."

Indeed, moving to the seaside tourist town, with a long-term goal of taking ownership of the antique shop once his grandfather had retired, had sounded ideal weeks ago, when Lucian's life had gone to hell from one day to the next.

The moan came again from the rear of the store. The sound of a soul in torment, the wail started softly and then rose in volume. "Ooooooooo…."

"That cry gives me the creeps." Galahad's puffed-up tail, swishing to and fro, resembled the fluffy duster stowed under the store counter.

Shaking his head, Lucian took a few backward steps and studied the watercolor in relation to the other artifacts around it. Light streaming in through the shop's long front windows shifted as people outside walked past. Thankfully, the passersby wouldn't be able to hear the Lady of the Plate's cries. Even if they caught some of Lucian and Galahad's conversation, they'd just hear a man talking to his cat, who had responded with meowing. Only the rare few gifted—or in Lucian and Galahad's case, cursed—with ancient magic could hear sounds made by magical items or understand what the feline was really saying.

"Ooooooooo…."

Galahad's ears flattened. "Can't you shut her up? Cats *do* have a far superior sense of hearing to humans."

That could well be true. However, Galahad was always claiming ways in which felines were far superior to their human masters.

"Grandfather said she doesn't cry for long." Moving forward, Lucian nudged the painting's right edge a little higher.

Galahad growled again. "Make her stop, or I might report you for torture of a Familiar."

*What?* Lucian frowned at the cat. "Don't be ridiculous."

The feline's eyes gleamed. "I am quite serious."

"I spoil you rotten. I feed you that expensive, organic cat food you like twice a day. You can eat dry kibble—"

"That looks like rabbit poop—"

"—whenever you like." Lucian scowled. "And I clean your litter box several times a day and brush you every morning."

Galahad started washing a front paw.

"You haven't puked up a single hairball since I started the brushing. And, as far as I know, you haven't had any more diarrhea or digestive issues—"

"God, Lucian!"

"—since you ate the ribbon around that stack of old postcards and I had to take you to the vet."

The cat averted his gaze. "You know I couldn't help what happened with the ribbon."

"You just *had* to gobble it down."

"Yes! It looked *so* enticing." Galahad sighed. "I wish I could explain how it called to me like a siren, seducing my willpower and—"

"Yeah, well, surely my rushing you to Dr. Anderson's clinic and paying the four-hundred-and-fifty dollar vet bill showed I care about your wellbeing?"

Galahad grumbled. "You are never going to let me forget that incident, are you?"

"Nope. And, you are never getting the chance to eat ribbon again."

"Sometimes, I can't stand to think that you and I are cursed to be together *forever*."

"Oooooooooo…."

"That's it!" The cat leapt down from the chair. "I'm going to break that damned plate. Then, she will be quiet."

"All right." The soles of Lucian's brogues squeaked on the hardwood floor as he swiveled to face the shelf and lifted his right hand, palm up. He focused his thoughts upon the exquisitely hand-painted Wagner plate portraying a beautiful, young woman with flowing brown hair and wide blue eyes.

"Shh," he silently commanded and curled his fingers inward, as though to catch and contain the sound.

The lady's mouth closed. Caught in Lucian's spell, her gaze became lifeless, as though there was no more to her than layers of paint on porcelain.

"Ahh," Galahad said. "Finally."

Lucian retrieved the etched stemware and figurines he'd moved from the shelf near the watercolor and set them back in their places. To be honest, the Lady of the Plate *had* gotten on his nerves, but because he pitied her. Like the gallant knight he'd once been centuries ago, before he'd been cursed, he hated to hear a woman in distress. The antique, like many others in the shop, bore the ghostly fragment of what had once been a flesh-and-blood person who'd died under tragic circumstances.

The first time he'd touched the plate, its provenance had flashed like snippets of film in his mind: the shrieking winds of a hurricane; an oak tree crashing through the roof of an upscale Florida home and crushing the screaming woman inside; and the plate, knocked by a branch onto a rug on the floor, intact but a silent witness to the tragedy.

When the woman had died, a piece of her soul had become connected to the antique. Most likely, she'd had a strong sentimental attachment to it.

"Would it be possible to wrap up the plate and ship it off to your brother's antiques store in London?" Galahad asked.

"You know we can't do that." Lucian picked up the hammer he'd used earlier. "Rules, remember? The curse became attached to the item here in Florida. So it belongs here in this store, with us."

Galahad stomped across the Persian carpet. "Well, thanks to Little Miss Moaning, my hopes of a much-needed afternoon nap have been destroyed. I'll be cranky for the rest of the day. *Not* my fault."

Lucian brushed cat hair off the Victorian chair. "Even if I could send the plate away, I wouldn't. Grandfather has quite a fondness for the young lady."

"Unfortunately," Galahad muttered.

"She's one of my favorites among those I call our long-term guests." Lucian's grandfather had encouraged him to take the plate from its lacquered display stand. "I got her from a guy who'd bought her shortly after Hurricane Andrew. Remember that storm back in 1992? It caused lots of damage in South Florida. Killed quite a few people, too."

The older man had taken the antique from Lucian. Gently, he'd set it back on its stand, in its assigned place on the shelf next to the Steiff teddy bear that had belonged to a mass murderer from Orlando; the music box that had concealed the chopped off pinkie of a former trapeze artist for the Ringling Brothers Circus; and other items tainted by magic. So many tagged and catalogued items of dark magic lined the back shelves, his grandfather could claim to have a small museum.

Carrying out a specific pattern of movements with his fingers, Lucian's grandfather had reinstalled the magical field around the plate. The field not only made the antique invisible to visitors to the store, but prevented the dark energy from influencing anything—or any*one*—in the normal world. It was among the safeguards required by The Experts, that all antiques brought into the store that possessed by evil magic had to be contained in that manner.

Lucian's gaze shifted to Galahad, now sitting in one of the front windows. "Next time, try to be patient with the Lady of the Plate, okay? She isn't to blame for her curse."

"Like you and I, my lord."

Galahad rarely bothered to address Lucian that way anymore. The formality between them had become irrelevant long ago.

Centuries ago.

How Lucian wished he could recall the battle with the sorceress that had made him and Galahad into who they were today. But, he had no memories beyond his lifetime as Lucian Lord.

Galahad, though, remembered everything. He'd said the fight had taken place when Lucian was a medieval lord and Galahad his squire. Lucian had rescued his betrothed from being burned alive by the sorceress trying to attain eternal life, but before the evil bitch had died, she'd placed a curse upon Lucian's bloodline.

Immediately after she'd perished, he'd been confronted by The Experts—a secret society of sorcerers of good magic—who had given him one choice: swear allegiance to them, or be destroyed. They wouldn't allow him to fall under the influence of the ambitious, evil Dealers of Darkness. Fearing he'd never see his lady love again, Lucian had taken the oath.

For centuries, Lucian had lived, died, and been reincarnated. Each lifetime had been spent as an antiques specialist with an interest in the Middle Ages who reported to The Experts. Galahad, who'd somehow been transformed into a cat when the sorceress tried to kill him, had also lived numerous lifetimes.

To be fifteen forever, trapped in a feline's body with all those raging teenage hormones….

Maybe Galahad had a right to be a little grouchy.

As the cat lay down in the sunshine, Lucian crossed to the store's oak counter and put away the hammer. Earlier, he'd started sorting through a box of silverware his grandfather had bought at auction and stored until he had time to tag the pieces. As his grandfather had done before purchasing the lot, Lucian had confirmed by running his hand over the silver that none of the pieces held dark magic and therefore could be sold to the general public.

As Lucian set an ornate serving spoon on the

counter, he thought of the gleaming cases of antique silver at the New England store. Until two months ago, he'd been the East Coast Representative for The Experts: a prestigious position. He'd screwed up, and had lost all that he'd worked for.

His jaw tightened on a flare of anger and disappointment while he tied the string of a white price tag around the spoon's handle.

"Now *there's* a lady I'd like to hear moan."

Lucian glanced up. A young woman wearing sunglasses stood outside the shop window, looking in.

He knew quite a few people in Cat's Paw Cove, but he didn't recognize her.

Wavy, blond hair brushed her bare shoulders. She wore a sleeveless white sundress, and as his gaze slid down her shapely curves, he saw the open cardboard box tucked under her left arm.

Was she a potential customer? Heat tingled in his gut; he hoped so.

"I saw her first," Galahad said, sounding petulant.

"True, but you're a cat."

To get a better look at Galahad, meowing and gazing up at her, she leaned closer to the window. The shift in posture brought the shadow of her cleavage into view. Lucian's hand curled against the counter's cool surface, for he longed to see more.

Reining in his stirring of interest, he forced his attention back to the silverware. She might be on her way to one of the other shops on the downtown street—not bringing items to his grandfather's store for a free evaluation. Lucian didn't want to be caught ogling, no matter how much her hourglass figure appealed to him. She might think him one of those antique dealer geeks who was starved for a woman's attention.

He wasn't starved. Single, yes. But, he'd never had a problem getting a date when he wanted one.

As he fastened a price tag around another piece of silver, though, he couldn't resist looking at her again. Shifting the box, she tapped on the glass and smiled at Galahad, who promptly rose to all fours and stretched to the tip of his tail.

*Show off.*

The woman's smile widened with delight.

How lovely she looked—

As she cooed to Galahad and leaned down even farther, something in the box shifted. Panic swept her features, and her free hand flew to keep items from falling out. Her sunglasses slipped from her nose.

Before Lucian realized he'd sprung into motion, he was halfway to the door.

"You *would* play chivalrous knight to the rescue," Galahad groused.

"Of course." Lucian pulled the wooden door open. A small bell attached to it chimed, a musical sound against the noise of the cars driving by on the street.

As he stepped outside, ninety-nine-degree heat washed over him. In the air-conditioned store, it was easy to forget just how scorching it could be in Florida. A shock-like tingle also raced through him, a sign he'd passed through the magical barrier his grandfather had set up around the premises—added protection in case a wily Dealer of Darkness decided to infiltrate the shop, or any of the dark magic artifacts tried to cause trouble.

Lucian hurried to the young woman. She crouched on the sidewalk, her skirt brushing the dirty concrete, the box in front of her. With careful hands, she felt the newspaper-wrapped items, as though checking nothing was broken. In the brilliant sunshine, her hair looked even more golden.

Either she hadn't heard the door open, or she was too concerned about breakage for her to acknowledge him right away. Looking down at her, he found himself in the perfect position to see what had been denied to him before. The shadowed valley of her cleavage was framed by the lacy white trim of her bra—

No. He was a gentleman. He wouldn't ogle—

A thudding noise intruded: Galahad, up on his hind legs and pawing on the other side of the glass.

A timely interruption.

"Is everything all right?" As Lucian crouched beside the woman, he caught a hint of her citrusy perfume.

Her shoulders--slopes of fair, satiny skin—tensed. Either she was reluctant to answer his question, or she'd only just become aware of him. Her long lashes flickered then she looked up at him. Her blue-eyed gaze held his before she looked back down at the box. "Oh, damn it," she muttered.

Lucian's excitement fizzled. Most women, when he talked to them, smiled. Many tried to prolong the conversation with flirting and touching his arm. Not once had a woman answered him by averting her gaze and cussing.

"Sorry. I didn't mean to be rude." She peered down at the box again. "I lost one of my contact lenses yesterday. It went down the bathroom sink, and I haven't had a chance to buy more." Her hand slid to the right. "My sunglasses are prescription. I know they fell in here somewhere—"

"Bottom right corner," Lucian said, just as her fingertips hit the tortoiseshell plastic frames.

Her shoulders dropped on a relieved sigh. "Thank you."

"My pleasure."

She pushed the sunglasses onto the bridge of her nose. Perspiration glistened on her face, and Lucian suddenly became aware of the sweat trickling down the back of his neck and under the collar of his polo shirt.

*Be a gentleman. Invite her in.*

When she picked up the box and rose, he stood as well.

Their gazes met again. As though seeing him for the first time, a pretty blush stained her cheekbones. Her gaze darted over his shirt that fit snugly enough to show off the muscles he'd built through intense workouts at the gym—the only way he'd kept his sanity through the turmoil of the past few months.

"Well." She sounded a little breathless. "Thank you so much for your help."

Lucian ignored the *thud* of Galahad's paws on the window again. "It's very hot out here." Good God, could he not have come up with something more inspiring to say?

"Yes, it is." Her expression turned rueful. "It's supposed to be a heat index of one-hundred-and-five today. I'm not used to such temperatures or the humidity."

Was she was a visitor to Florida? To Cat's

Paw Cove? He must find out.

As she wiped her brow with the back of her hand, Lucian managed his most charming smile. He gestured to the shop's open door. "Why don't you come in for a moment and cool off?"

Read the rest of Lucian and Molly's story in Catherine Kean's book *Hot Magic*, available Tuesday, November 19 in eBook and print.

## Also available from Cat's Paw Cove

In a violent storm in 1645, Colin Wilshire's Barbados-bound ship is swept off course. He's sure he and his pregnant bride are fated to drown when he's tossed into the sea. He wakes in a strange land and is saved by a blue-haired angel.

Twenty-first-century witch and cat rescuer Luna Halpern has fallen for more than her share of unsuitable guys—including one with a long-distance fiancé, and another who was more interested in other dudes than in Luna. Finally, a safe, drama-free guy is interested in her, and she's confident that she'll muster up an attraction to him. When she stumbles upon a handsome, mysterious man who speaks oddly, seems not to know where he is, or even what century it is, her first instinct is to help him.

Certain he's either stuck in a crazy dream or in limbo between life and death, Colin stays close to Luna. As his feelings for her grow, he's forced to choose between his obligations in the past and his hopes for the future.

Available in eBook, print, and audio book.

Also available from Cat's Paw Cove

Event Planner and earthly Cupid Tori Sutherland enjoys nothing more than playing matchmaker for lonely hearts. Too bad Tori will never find her own happy-ever-after because the only guy she ever loved moved on years ago.

Heath Castillo managed to escape his dysfunctional family for a career in major-league baseball. His only regret was not acting upon his desire for his best friend. When an injury threatens his livelihood, Heath has no choice but to face the ghosts of his past.

When long-buried passions ignite, Heath and Tori consider taking a chance on love. But will the forces that kept them apart in high school destroy their budding romance before it even begins?
her, tall, dark, and handsome help enters the shop just in the nick of time.

Available in eBook and print.

## Coming Tuesday, November 5
## from Cat's Paw Cove

Eight holiday tales set in the magical town of Cat's Paw Cove:

FAMILIAR BLESSINGS
by Candace Colt
To repay an old man who brought him out of war's dark shadow, a former Army Ranger delivers a cryptic letter to a gifted medium in Cat's Paw Cove. If what the letter says is true, the reluctant medium and skeptical Ranger must travel back to 1720 to save a young boy from the gallows.

CHRISTMAS AT MOON MIST MANOR by Kerry Evelyn
Lanie and Matt Saunders return to Cat's Paw Cove two years after their first disastrous Christmas there. When a mysterious kitten leads Matt back in time, can he right the wrongs of the past and give his expectant wife the perfect Christmas?

CHARLOTTE REDBIRD: GHOST COACH
by Sharon Buchbinder
With the help of hunky real estate agent, Dylan Graham, life coach Charly Redbird and her new kitten have found the perfect home next to a cemetery. Charly gets a new client right away, who happens to

be her neighbor—and a ghost. What could possibly go wrong?

GNOME FOR THE HOLIDAYS
by Kristal Hollis
When an empath who's failed at every relationship impulsively kisses an enchanted garden gnome, he magically turns into a real man. Together they must find his one true love and end the curse by Christmas or he'll be forever alone and trapped within his stone prison.

RING MA BELL
by Debra Jess
In 1979, Michael Bell fell in love with high seas radio technician Dvorah Levi's voice as she guided him to safety, but their marriage was cut short by a bullet. Forty years later, Dvorah still mourns him. Can a special holiday and a magical Sherwood cat bring him back?

PURRFECTLY CHRISTMAS
by Mia Ellas
Faerie Sormey Johnson moved to Cat's Paw Cove to live a quiet life as a human until a sexy werewolf deputy needs her help tracking down a murderous monster. When Sormey offers herself as bait, the cost may be more than she bargained for.

COLLYWOBBLES FOR CHRISTMAS
by Sue-Ellen Welfonder
The fate of star-crossed lovers falls into the magical paws of a time-traveling kitten determined to right an ancient wrong and claim the greatest Christmas gift of

all - love.

NEW YEAR'S KISS
by Darcy Devlon
In order to overcome a family curse, Griffin Brooks, the town's hotshot assistant fire chief, must earn his true love's trust. Trina Lancaster knows she can release Griffin's curse, but will her magical family baggage be a deal breaker?

Available in eBook and print.

# About Wynter Daniels

Bestselling author Wynter Daniels has written more than three dozen romances, including contemporary, romantic suspense, and paranormal romance books for several publishers including Entangled Publishing and Carina Press as well as for Kristen Painter's Nocturne Falls Universe.

In 2019, she started CPC Publishing with author Catherine Kean.

She lives in sunny Florida with her family and a rescue cat named Chloe (who thinks she is dog, and tries all day to distract Wynter from writing).

Wynter loves to keep in touch with her readers! Please follow her on the following sites:

**Website**
https://www.wynterdaniels.com/

**Facebook**
https://www.facebook.com/wynter.daniels

**BookBub**
https://www.bookbub.com/search?search=Wynter+Daniels

**Goodreads**
https://www.goodreads.com/author/show/3521407.
Wynter_Daniels

**Instagram**
https://www.instagram.com/wynterdaniels/

**Amazon Page**
https://www.amazon.com/Wynter-
Daniels/e/B003U2KQCM/

Made in the USA
San Bernardino, CA
27 July 2019